AMERICAN TROPIC

THOMAS SANCHEZ

American
Tropic

ALFRED A. KNOPF 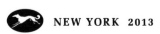 NEW YORK 2013

Grateful acknowledgment is made to David Platz Music Inc. for permission to reprint an excerpt from "First Time Ever I Saw Your Face" by Ewan MacColl. Copyright © by David Platz Music Inc. All rights reserved. Used by permisson of David Platz Music Inc.

Library of Congress Cataloging-in-Publication Data
Sanchez, Thomas.
American tropic / by Thomas Sanchez. — 1st ed.
p. cm.
"This is a Borzoi book."
ISBN 978-1-4000-4232-6
1. Murder—Fiction. 2. Key West (Fla.)—Fiction. 3. Suspense fiction. I. Title.
PS3569.A469A83 2013
813'.54—dc23   2012035328

Jacket photograph by Brian Pieters/Masterfile
Jacket design by Wednesday Design

Manufactured in the United States of America

First Edition

For Geraldine Louise
my mother, whose inspiration
sent the first words sailing . . .
to the dove over the ocean
her spread of wings
forming a perfect A
for Astrid
and for
Ash Green,
hand at the helm.

American tropic islands . . .
that true poetic spirit that
can find inspiration in
humble and even vulgar things;
that, furthermore, can draw from low nature
and her commonplaces
deep lessons for human life.

—FROM A RUMINATION ON THE POET OF
THE REVOLUTION, *ATLANTIC MONTHLY,* 1904

ACKNOWLEDGMENTS

Shelter from the storm,
Robert Mailer Anderson & Nicola Miner
Cecelia Joyce & Seward Johnson
Jean-Leo Gros.

AMERICAN TROPIC

Where the brooding Atlantic meets the moody torrent of the Gulf Stream, water and darkness give birth to the rip tides of fate roaring up through murky underwater canyons. Far above, on the ocean's roiling dark surface, the silhouette of a lone boat heaves on waves. Bolted to its upper deck is a sturdy metal radio-transmitter antenna. From the transmitter an insistent male voice broadcasts. The words ride, invisible, through the air from east to west. They can be heard from the Great Bahama Bank all the way to the distant island of Cuba. They travel wide across the ocean, from the Tropic of Cancer to the island of Key West, off the coast of Florida. The words become an urgent question.

"Is

        anyone

                out

                        there?"

The question hangs, the words stop, then they begin again, rhythmically rising in a strident drumbeat.

"This is Truth Dog broadcasting from pirate-radio boat *Noah's Lark* to the whole dead world, speaking to you out of the darkness of night. Are there two brains out there to rub together for a spark of illumination? Do you hear me? Maybe no one is awake in Key West, just twenty miles across the water from me. Maybe all the eyes on that coral-capped island are closed to the obvious truth. Perhaps no one is awake in the wide world that spins obliviously toward its own demise. Could be

I'm floating out here alone, broadcasting to a country of unliving people caught in a zombie stupor of collective historical amnesia and collapsed moral hearts. Could be that only the fish beneath me in the sea are awake, sliding through opaque waters, finning through submerged canyons carved by millennia of time, their mouths agape, fins pushing against water's gravity, on the prowl for their next meal, dead between their eyes to any joy, propelled by their simple ancient truth of gut survival.

"Hey, dead-between-the-eyes fish zombies! Call me now. I'm on the line for you. I'm on the hook. I'm like God in the heavens, or Jesus in the confessional box, or Moses in the lightning glow on the mountaintop. Better yet, I take calls from sinners and seekers, repenters and fakers.

"Call me before it is too late. Wake up, little zombies, wake up. Call even if you are dead and only now are awakening in the afterlife, your cold fish-scaled bodies slithering out of the sea onto the shore of a new beginning in an old world. Call Truth Dog, an old dog with new tricks.

"Call me and tell me how the lightning on the mountaintop strikes you between those dead eyes of yours so you see illuminated the green flash of light across the ocean's horizon spelling out a new dawn and you can finally shout the truth.

"Illumination.

Illuminate or die.

Show me your rage."

Luz awakens in her bed from dreams of deep-indigo oceans. Her brown eyes take in the white-skinned body of Joan sleeping next to her. Joan's blond hair lies spread over the pillow; her deep breathing heaves the curve of her bare breasts in a rhythmic rise and fall that Luz has known intimately for twelve years. Luz kisses Joan's bare shoulder and slides her dark hand below the white swell of one of Joan's breasts. Luz stares at her hand, her fingers in a winged shape, a dark bird flying beneath the full orb of an alabaster moon.

Above the bed, the ceiling fan's blades swirl through the humid air. The insistent sound brings Luz back from her brief flight to Joan's fleshy landscape. She looks up wide-eyed at the blades as their slicing sound grows louder, as forceful as incoming surf crashing onto an island, waves smashing, spraying, drowning everything, plunging Luz back beneath an indigo ocean, where she swims in watery turmoil surrounded by mysterious creatures lurking in a fathomless deep.

Luz shakes her head, driving submerged images from her mind. She turns quickly away from the fan's blades. She rises from her bed and stands barefoot before her dresser, her white cotton underwear tight against the sheen of her dark skin. She dresses quickly in black pants and a white Cuban-style guayabera shirt. From the dresser top she picks up a loaded Glock 30 semiautomatic pistol with a thick gorilla-grip handle. She snaps the heavy black weapon into its leather holster on a belt. She lifts the long shirt above her pants and straps the gun snug against her waist. She glances into the mirror above the dresser. The mirror reflects Joan's naked blondness on the bed behind, superimposed over the image of her own shadow-skinned reflection. She drops her loose shirt over the pistol holstered at her hip and looks closely at herself in the mirror. Her black hair is cropped short; her smooth facial features are natural, devoid of any makeup; her eyes hold a steady gaze and do not blink.

Luz leaves Joan sleeping in the bedroom and walks with quiet steps down a narrow dark hallway to a closed door. She pushes the door silently open and looks in on two teenaged girls asleep in separate beds. The older is a healthy sixteen-year-old; her untroubled breath is even, her lips are curved in a smile. In the opposite bed is a younger girl, of fourteen, her bone-thin body pallid and hairless from chemotherapy treatments fighting her childhood leukemia. Next to her bed is a wheelchair, and a nightstand covered with medicine bottles. She stirs awake; her eyes open slowly, with painful effort. She smiles at the sight of Luz. Luz puts her fingers to her lips and blows the girl a kiss, then softly shuts the bedroom door.

In her living room, Luz kneels before a walnut-wood Spanish chest. The top of the chest is commanded by a tall ceramic statue of a Black Madonna. The Madonna holds in her arms an infant child with a beatific smile etched on its face. Luz strikes a match and lights a candle in a red glass holder in front of the statue. She clasps her hands together in a pointed prayerful position. She looks straight into the Madonna's soulful eyes as she whispers her prayer.

"As a mother myself, I beseech you to take pity on my daughters, Nina and Carmen. Cure my little Nina of her cancer and suffering. Only you, holiest of all mothers, can stop the pain of an innocent child. Give me the strength to protect my daughters and my beloved, Joan. Give me the strength to do what I must do to keep my family safe from the evil that surrounds them."

Luz's misty eyes focus on the candle flame flickering in front of the Madonna. The flame sparkles and burns stronger, transforming into a brilliant glow.

A red rising sun emerges on the ocean's dark horizon. Out of the sun flies a winged armada of seabirds. The birds swoop down from the sky over the water's surface. They glide above the humped shell of a large sea turtle below. The turtle's green front fins stroke through the blue, propelling the primeval creature's bulk relentlessly forward. The birds pass on; beneath them, dolphins break the sea's surface. The dolphins' sleek wet bodies arch out of the water into the air in a dazzling, twisting spray. They then dive back out of sight. Impervious to the dolphins, the birds sail on over the dark saucer-shaped shadows of giant stingrays just below the ocean's skin. The birds continue their journey over open water. They suddenly bank hard, whooshing the air as they descend in a wing-flapping circle around a channel-marker buoy afloat below.

The large anchored buoy's wide platform base sloshes in the water. Rising up from the base is a tall metal pole with an orange plastic star-shaped reflector at its peak.

The reflector glints with shards of orange light. A dead man's naked body is tied by a thick knotted rope to the pole. Slashed on the body's abdomen is a painted red **X**. A steel spear is pierced through the man's chest. From below the spear a stream of blood has hardened into a congealed purple crust. The white lips of the man's blood-drained face have been sewn crudely shut with fishing line. His ears have been cut off, leaving two gashed holes. The orbs of the man's eyes remain open. The eyes stare off across the distance of the ocean. In death, the eyes seem fixed on a horror that the sewn-up lips cannot scream the name of.

etween the islands of Key West and Cuba, the sun's globe rises into the sky above a weather-beaten 1950s West Indian Heritage trawler. The anchored boat sways in a watery blue canyon created by the rise and fall of waves. On the bow of its thirty-six-foot-long hull is painted the name *Noah's Lark.* A twelve-foot-high steel radio-transmitter antenna is bolted to the deck. Inside the windowed pilothouse is a jerry-rigged radio-broadcasting control room. Seated on a ragged swivel chair in front of a console of outdated analog equipment is a man wearing a sun-faded seersucker suit that hangs loosely on his angular frame. His sleep-deprived reddened eyes stare intensely at the console's flickering red and green lights. The lines etched deeply into the man's face convey a hard life lived. He agitatedly fingers the bearded stubble of his unshaven chin, then clamps on a pair of battered earphones over the unruly hair of his head. He pulls in close to the metal stub of a microphone on the table before him. His lips loosen with a quiver as if about to deliver a kiss to an unseen lover. His melodious voice suddenly cracks open the morning silence with a basso swagger.

"Rise and shine, all of you in the Florida Keys about to lose your paradise. Rub the stars out of your eyes and take your brains out of your shoes. Today's temps are soaring up to ninety-nine degrees, too hot to wear your own sweat, let alone your lover's sweat. This is Noah Sax, your very own Truth Dog, broadcasting from international waters over Conch Pirate Radio offshore from Key West. Key West, Cayo Hueso, Island of Bones—that was the name the early Spanish explorers gave the place when they found it littered with nothing but the bleached remains of the hounded, deserted, and luckless. The Spaniards beat it. Key West, America's southernmost continental point, where the Overseas Highway ends after hopping across bridges linking forty-three islands on its one-hundred-thirty-mile run down from Miami. Key West, last American island, end of the road at the famous sign, MILE MARKER ZERO. As the poet once wrote, nowhere to go from mile zero except to swim with the sharks and barracuda. Which is where I am, floating with the sharks and barracuda far out at sea, where the feds can't stop my pirate radio beaming the truth across the open ocean.

"Nowhere does the bell of accountability ring out so loudly as here in the Florida Keys. This fragile ecosystem is dotted with coral-and-mangrove-entwined islands guarded by the third-largest coral reef in the world and the only living coral reef in North America. The fragrant salty air that you breathe here so freely must be defended at all costs, before these islands are covered over in the oil-pollution slime that greases the implacable wheel of man-made environmental destruction. Don't fool with Mother Nature or Mother Nature will fool with you!"

Noah's words stop. He grabs a rum bottle from next to his microphone and takes a swig. He swipes the liquid from his lips and continues.

"I'm out here on the open sea in the sun, unlike Internet bloggers hunkered down in solitary dark holes. My old-school live radio is stand-up accountability. I'm the only eco-shock jock broadcasting at sea, letting you, my irreverent audience, roar your disgust against the destruction of the environment. Your words are bullets, so aim straight. Call Noah now, punch me with the power of your pain and pissed-off kisses. If you're a cynic, comic, or crusader, join the chorus of the committed. Dial Five-Five-C-O-N-C-H. Act out, act up, but act. I'm here for you. I'm a lightning rod, shoot me your lightning. Rock the world with thunder. Show me your rage!"

Noah clutches the microphone in his trembling hand and holds it close to his mouth. He leans back in his chair, takes a deep breath, and switches to a mellow tone.

"While you're getting ready to put your sweet lips to the phone, let me serve you a hot cup of morning *amore*, get you in the mood with a beat brewed by our Cuban neighbors just ninety miles across the ocean."

Noah punches one of the buttons on the broadcast console, starting a CD player wired to a pair of battered wooden speakers. A full-orchestra salsa beat from the speakers fills the pilothouse with an insistent throb. Noah closes his eyes and sways to the seductive rhythm. He gets up from his chair. His arms reach out to an invisible partner, and he dances in a hip-strutting glide around the pilothouse.

Outside Noah's anchored trawler, the sound of salsa cuts sharp as a musical knife across the ocean's surface. With nothing to stop it, the music can be heard in the far distance to where a raft drifts. The raft is constructed from scraps of wood crudely lashed with fraying rope. Its sail is a patchwork of fabric stitched together. The ragged sail flaps forlornly in the slight breeze from a broken wood mast. Strewn across the raft are the sun-blackened bodies of men, women, and children. Their arms and legs are akimbo in grotesque contortions of death, the flesh peeling from their bodies, exposing white bones. Their eyes have been pecked out by marauding birds.

In a morning-bright kitchen, Joan at the stove hums cheerfully as she cooks breakfast. At the table, Luz watches her sixteen-year-old daughter, Carmen, brushing toucan-beak-orange-colored polish onto her fingers.

Luz shakes her head at Carmen. "Are you getting ready to go to school or to a nightclub?"

Carmen looks up, her long straight brown hair framing her face. She smiles. "Mom, I'm getting straight A's."

Joan turns from her pots and pans steaming on the stovetop and shoots Carmen a reassuring wink. "That's right, honey, you keep trotting those A's home and you can paint your nails any color you want. How about painting each one a different color? Be bold."

Luz loosens her stern gaze. "Okay, I get it. A's equal painted fingernails. I'll go with that, but no lipstick. I don't want my girl wearing lipstick to school. It's not acceptable in this family."

Carmen screws the cap onto the nail-polish bottle and picks up her textbooks from the table. She gets up and kisses Luz on the cheek. "You win, Mom. No lipstick. I'm off."

"And no tricks. Don't put a ton of lipstick on when you get out of the house. Promise me."

Carmen hugs Luz. "Promise, Mom. Jeez, no lipstick."

Luz watches Carmen leave, the door closing behind. She notices Carmen's plate of uneaten food on the table. "Left without eating again. She's too skinny. Got to fatten her up on rice and beans and *ropa vieja.*"

Joan hands Luz a cup of coffee. "Don't be so hard on her. She's a good girl."

"Carmen's goodness is not what worries me. It's the world out there around her that bothers me." Luz takes a sip of coffee. The wrinkled look of concern across her smooth face doesn't go away.

Joan nudges her playfully. "You were a wild teenager. Drove the boys crazy. You got knocked up when you were eighteen."

"Nineteen, and it wasn't boys, you know that, it was one guy. Twice he got me pregnant, I married him like a good Cuban girl—you know the story."

"Sorry, hon, didn't mean to bring that up. We won't talk about him."

"No, we don't speak of the beast with no name. Story over."

"But look at you now. A pillar of society, an officer of the law, and a cute one at that." Joan strokes Luz's short black hair and sings with a throaty purr, "In the jungle, the mighty jungle, my panther prowls for me."

Luz tilts her head back; her worried expression fades as her brown eyes gaze up at Joan.

Joan's hands caress Luz's arched neck. "You want to fool around, panther?"

"You know I can't on a workday."

Joan leans over; her blond hair cascades around Luz as she whispers, "We could fool around and fool around and fall in love."

"We are in love, my darling."

Joan's fingers deftly open the top buttons of Luz's shirt; her hands slip onto Luz's exposed skin.

Luz grips Joan's wrists, pulling Joan's hands away. Joan's jaw tightens; her lips draw into a tight line.

Luz rebuttons her shirt and gazes with concern around the kitchen. "Why isn't Nina here? Where's Nina?"

"Don't be such a cop on the job all the time. Nina is fine. She wants to get herself ready for school. She needs to be independent."

Luz shoves her chair away from the table and leaves. She walks quickly down a hallway and pushes open a bedroom door. She looks inside.

Nina sits in her wheelchair before a dresser with a large mirror. Her fourteen-year-old body is frail, her torso shrunken, her head bald from chemotherapy. She turns around to Luz, her large brown eyes still luminous. "Mom, I'm glad you're here. I need your opinion."

"About what, baby?"

Nina holds out two long wigs, one blond, one brunette. She studies the wigs critically. "Who should I look like today? Marilyn Monroe or Cleopatra?"

"Show me both wigs so I can judge."

Nina puts on the blond wig and purses her lips in a sophisticated pout. "What about Marilyn? Am I as irresistible as her?"

"Marilyn never looked so good. Maybe it's a bit too much for school—but you look great."

Nina pulls off the blond wig and puts on the brunette. She gives a sassy stare. "Am I as powerful as Cleo?"

"Yes, you've definitely got the Queen Cleo vibe going."

"Mom, you can't be such a pushover and like both wigs. Help me. Which one?"

Luz steps close to Nina in the wheelchair. She picks up the blond wig and pulls it on over her cropped black hair. She stares at her reflection in the dresser mirror. The light-colored wig contrasts sharply with the darkness of her face. Luz mugs a sultry expression. "Do you think I'm sexy?"

"Mom, you're such a goof."

Luz leaves the wig on. "Come on, do you think I'm sexy?"

"No. I think you're funny."

"I think I'm sexy."

Nina studies Luz in the blond wig. "Okay, yes, you're crazy nutzoid sexy!" Nina's frail body shakes with laughter.

Luz pulls off the blond wig. "Baby, I've got to go to work."

"Which wig should I wear, Mom?"

Luz wraps her arms around Nina and holds her tight, then strokes her smooth bald head. "I want my girl as she already is. Shining more beautiful than Marilyn on the silver screen. Braver than Cleopatra on her war boat."

Far out on the ocean, the recorded beat of salsa music ends inside the pilothouse of Noah's pirate-radio boat. He stops his dancing with an invisible partner. He sits back down on the worn chair in front of the makeshift broadcasting console.

Noah speaks rapidly into the microphone. "I still don't have any calls from my intrepid pilgrims out there. If you don't want to show me the rage, let's talk about the Power-boat Championship Race starting from Key West Harbor this morning. Those boats burn enough fuel in one race to fly a jumbo jet across the Atlantic. Hey, let's not sweat the carbon emissions. Let's disregard a monstrous guzzle of fossil fuel from the tit of Mother Earth when the scent of blood sport is in the air. Today, Key West's native-son racer, Dandy Randy, is set to break his own speed record of more than ninety miles an hour. Problem is, Randy went missing after yesterday's qualifying race. Where's Randy? Holed up in a poker parlor? Adrift in puke after a night of prowling sleazy bars? At the bottom of the sea, entangled in a net with dead turtles? What's up with Randy? What's up with the turtle slaughter? Sea turtles are being killed by gill nets and long hook-lines by the millions. Show me the rage!"

In front of Noah, on the console's instrument panel, three cell phones are wired into battered wood speakers. A light flashes red on one of the phones, signaling an incoming call.

Noah presses the answer button. "I've reeled in my first caller. I hope you're a whopper."

A male voice booms from the speakers. "Hey, Truth Dog, I've been listening since you started your pirate-radio gig a year ago. You're so righteous to call out those macho joystick powerboat racers like Candy Bambi."

"Dandy Randy."

"Whatever. Were you around back in the eighties, when Key West was Dodge City on the Gulf Stream? Totally lawless time, cocaine smuggling and high jinks par *excellente*!"

"I was getting my degree in environmental law up in Miami then, but Key West has always been a pirate island, stolen treasures off of wrecked ships lured by false lights onto the reef offshore, rumrunners, gunrunners, drug runners, any kind of contraband. What ruined your little paradise?"

"Not the smuggling. It's that Key West isn't a fishing port anymore. The shrimpers and their boats were kicked out to put in seaside condos. Hordes of tourists driving down here on the Overseas Highway. Giant cruise ships spitting out thousands of passengers. It's the tourists who are killing the coral reef offshore of Key West."

"Now you're showing some rage. But tourists, you think they're killing America's only continental reef? You think they're killing a two-hundred-forty-million-year-old reef?"

"Hell, yeah!"

"No! Coral die-off is caused by the thermal stress of ocean warming. Added to this is the ocean dumping of toxic pesticides and chemicals. I want to expose the real culprits. I want to peel the lies off of their greedy hides, the same way the shark hunters used to knife-skin a shark with a one-bladed stroke. The reefs are the rain forests of the sea. Fifty percent of the Caribbean reefs are already dead because of warming, pollution, and net-fishing ships. Soon every coral reef on earth will be dead!"

Noah punches off the caller and clicks on another phone. "I can't hear you, talk louder, there's static on the line."

A belligerent voice echoes through the static. "I want you to know, I'm a vet. I was in Vietnam."

"Is that supposed to be a cause for celebration or condemnation?"

"Fuck you!"

"Now that we've got that out of the way, I'm all ears."

"Perm . . . ian Ex . . . tinc . . . tion E . . . vent."

"Permian Extinction Event? What's that got to do with anything? Happened millions of years ago. A volcanic methane-gas explosion that wiped out nearly every living thing on our planet."

"It's also called the Great Dying. It's what you've been quackin' about and you don't even see the connection. It's comin' again."

"Okay, Nam vet, I'm on the edge of my seat. Shoot me facts."

"This time the explosion of obliteration will be man-made."

"What's the trigger? Nuclear war?"

"It's comin' from beneath the boat you're floatin' on, from the seafloor of the Gulf of Mexico."

"And you say it's man-made. So I figure you must mean that—"

A thundering boom comes from outside Noah's trawler. He looks through the window of the pilothouse. The radio-transmitter antenna bolted to the deck sways. The trawler rocks hard from side to side. Noah tries to keep the shaking electronic equipment on the broadcast console from falling. He catches his rum bottle as it tumbles from the table. He glances around, trying to figure out what happened. He looks down through the window and sees that a drifting raft has collided with his trawler.

The raft is filled with a jumble of dead bodies. From among the bodies a bone-thin teenaged boy, shirtless and barefoot, rises. His black skin is sun-blistered and riddled with lacerations. The whites of his startled eyes loom large as he stares up at Noah in the pilothouse.

Noah yanks the ship-to-shore radio mike from its holder and shouts: "Mayday! This is *Noah's Lark*! Mayday!"

A gray sixty-foot-long Coast Guard cutter tows the small wooden raft with dead bodies toward Key West Harbor. Noah follows the cutter in his trawler. The cutter slows to a stop. Noah motors along-side and shouts to a uniformed guardsman on the cutter's deck, "What's the holdup?"

The guardsman shouts down, "Harbor's blocked, pow-erboat race starting, have to wait before going in."

Noah cuts his engine. He sees around him an an-chored flotilla of fancy yachts, paint-blistered skiffs, sleek ketches, and listing lobster boats crowded with beer-drinking revelers waiting for the spectacle to begin.

From the harbor's distant shoreline a cannon booms, signaling the race start. Cheers go up from the anchored flotilla. A roar of jet-propelled engines vibrates the air. Twelve long-hulled powerboats emerge from the harbor entrance. The waterborne herd thunders at full throttle, their boldly painted hulls nosed high, sharp bows tilt-ing six feet into the air, their rear exhausts blasting water up behind them. Deep within the cocooned cock-pits bolts of sunlight reflect off the driver's and throttle-man's crash helmets. The boats race in front of Noah's trawler with an earsplitting engine snarl; white-hot jet exhausts plow a showering spray. Above the powerboats a TV news helicopter chases the action. From the copter's open doorway a cameraman leans out, filming the boats as they roar toward the ocean's distant horizon and over its edge.

Noah's boat rocks in the watery wake left behind by the powerboats. The Coast Guard cutter's engines rev to a turbine whine. Noah follows the cutter towing the raft. Inside the harbor's anchorage, the cutter slows to a stop, and guardsmen secure it alongside a cement pier. Noah steers his boat around the cutter and ties up behind the raft. He watches through his pilothouse window as a crowd gathers on the pier, gawking at the sight of the raft with its cargo of bodies.

Among the crowd is Hogfish, straddling a rusty bicycle. From the back of his sun-faded fisherman's cap hangs a ragged swag of graying hair. IPhone earbuds are jammed into his ears. A tight T-shirt on his bony chest reads DON'T KILL THE MESSENGER. A queer grin spreads over his forty-year-old face, remarkable for its smooth, unlined quality. Only his bulging eyes, washed of all color and seeming to spin in opposite orbits, indicate a man burned out from battles fought in distant wars. Between the handlebars of his bicycle is stretched a fishing line, dangling with barbed J-hooks. He pushes the bicycle's front wheel against the taut rope mooring the raft to the dock.

A bullnecked deputy detective with a slick sunburnt shaved head, Moxel, shoves through the crowd to Hogfish. A shiny badge is pinned to his crisp blue uniform shirt. His lips carry the arrogant expression of a young man barging through life based on a combination of brute force and triumph over his low social origins. He grips the handlebars of Hogfish's bicycle above the line of dangling fishhooks and snarls in a Southern accent: "Get away from that rope. This is a crime scene."

Hogfish's head bobs to the clash of heavy-metal guitars playing through his old-model iPhone's earbuds. He pushes his front bicycle wheel harder against the rope to get a closer look at the grotesque scene in the raft.

Moxel tightens his fists on the handlebars of Hogfish's bicycle. "I'm talking to you! Back off! Didn't you hear me? Take out your goddamn earplugs!" Hogfish's head keeps bobbing.

Luz, dressed in her dark pants and guayabera shirt,

steps quickly through the crowd and grabs the scraggly ponytail hanging from behind Hogfish's fishing cap. The muscles in her arm tighten as she tugs the ponytail, pulling him away from the rope. She leans into his face and shouts, *"Dios da sombrero a quien no tiene cabeza!"*

Moxel elbows Luz and sneers. "What the hell does that mean?"

"God gives hats to some who have no head."

"Why not just say it in English? Your kind are always trying to make this a Spanish-speaking country."

Luz ignores Moxel and steps to a guardsman protecting the raft with a rifle clutched in his hands. The guardsman nervously holds up the rifle, blocking Luz. "Ma'am, you'll have to stay on the other side of the rope. This is official Coast Guard business. No one goes on the raft."

Luz pulls out her wallet, flips it open, and flashes her silver badge. "I'm Detective Luz Zamora, Key West Homicide. This dock is city property. I've got jurisdiction here, not the Coast Guard. I'm boarding the raft."

The guardsman looks at the badge and stands aside. "Yes, ma'am!"

Luz steps over the rope onto the edge of the concrete bulwark. She winces at the rotting stench drifting up from the bloated bodies. She jumps down onto the raft and moves quickly among the jumble of dead people, feeling the wrists of stiffened arms for a pulse.

A siren wails from the dock. The crowd parts for the arriving ambulance. The side door swings open; a paramedic hurries out. He jumps onto the raft and shouts at Luz above the still-wailing siren, "Is anyone alive?"

Luz turns to the paramedic. "No one. All dead."

The medic gazes in astonishment at the bodies on the

raft. He looks back at Luz. "Must be hard for you, seeing your people end up this way."

"What do you mean, my people?"

"You're Cuban. These are Cuban boat people."

"These people aren't Cubans, they're Haitians. But that doesn't make it less horrifying."

Luz looks away from the bodies. She sees Noah on the fly deck of his trawler, docked next to the raft. She calls over to him, "What do you know about this?"

Noah shouts back, "The raft was adrift, banged into my boat. I called in the Mayday."

Noah turns from Luz and goes back into his pilothouse. He grabs his bottle of rum off the console table. He walks over to a canvas curtain covering a storage closet in the corner. He pulls the curtain back, exposing the teenaged survivor from the raft. The boy appears terrified. Noah speaks softly in French: "Don't worry, I'll protect you. We've got to keep you hidden. If they find you, they'll send your sorry ass back to Haiti." He drinks rum from his bottle and looks sympathetically at the trembling boy. "Kid, you crossed seven hundred miles of shark-infested ocean to escape an earthquake-racked country of poverty, disease, and violence. Now you've got to do the hardest thing, you've got to trust me."

The boy mumbles in French, "My . . . name . . . is Rimbaud."

Noah responds in French. "What's the family name?"

"Mesrine."

Noah guzzles down the last of the rum and fixes the boy with a glassy-eyed philosophical expression. "Rimbaud Mesrine, damnedest thing. They named you after a famous gunrunning poet and a famous cold-blooded killer. They must have figured you were going to become a French politician."

Noah turns and looks down through the salt-streaked window of the pilothouse. He sees Luz on the raft moving among the dead bodies and speaks to her in words he knows she can't hear:

"Slaves and masters. Fucked up as it ever was."

Five miles out to sea from Key West, the twelve powerboats roar across the ocean's surface at ninety miles an hour. The TV news helicopter overhead chases the boats as they make a turn around a large channel marker. They speed away from the floating buoy. The copter hovers over it. The side door of the copter slides open, and a cameraman looks down, shocked at what he sees, almost losing his grip on the heavy camera as he shouts back at the pilot. "Damn! It's what I thought! Can't believe it!"

The copter's blades whip the air as the cameraman leans perilously out from the doorway. He aims his lens down and films the naked body of a dead man tied by rope to the buoy's metal pole.

The downward force of wind from the copter's blades above the body creates a churning circle in the water around the buoy. The copter pulls up and banks away. The buoy rocks in the watery wake left behind. The mutilated body tied to the pole sways beneath a relentless sun.

The Bounty Bar faces the boat-filled Key West Harbor. The walls are hung with an array of seafaring artifacts, big-game fishing rods and reels and colorful mounted trophy fish caught in their plasticized death leaps. The humid air moves in a rush from ceiling fans spinning over the heads of sport fishermen, shrimpers, real-estate hustlers, deadbeats, lushes, lowlifes, and wide-eyed tourists wearing floral-print shirts.

Commanding the scene from behind the long mahogany bar counter is Zoe. She emanates an effortless sophisticated beauty cut by a savvy aura of understanding the world of men. She moves quickly, with the calculated feline grace of knowing her ability to land securely no matter what situation she is thrown into. She pulls two bottles of beer up from the icy water of the large bright-red cooler and bangs them down on the counter in front of two Bounty Bar regulars, Big Conch and Hard Puppy.

Big Conch's cocked-up stature comes from the years when he outran Coast Guard cutters in his cocaine-packed cigarette boat across low-tide coral inlets. His face registers the righteousness of an outlaw who cashed out of his scam before being busted and left to rot in a federal slammer. His gray hair is dyed an unnatural blond hue and is slicked back flat against his scalp. Around Big's neck dangles the circular gold weight of Spanish medallions. His blue-eyed stare is that of a thug feigning a legit life in a new world of real-estate pimps and condo hustlers. He grabs the beer bottle in front of him and ham-fists it to his lips, sucking out the foaming brew.

Next to Big, Hard Puppy takes a slow, cool drink from his bottle. Hard is descended from a line of black Bahamian freemen who were once the property of British Caribbean overlords. He is outfitted in a flashy white silk suit and white alligator shoes, befitting his position as the number-one cash kingpin of illegal dogfighting from Key West to Miami. Around Hard floats in the air the lime scent of aftershave lotion that he slaps onto his sharp-featured face every day to keep away the scent of poverty he grew up with and that he always smells: the stink of unchanged shit in diapers and a drunk stepfather snoring on top of his puked-out, passed-out mother.

Hard and Big straighten up on their stools to get a better view of Zoe behind the bar. They admire her long tanned legs captured by tight white shorts and, above that, a thin strategic halter top offering the right amount of provocative glimpse of her breasts.

Big glances at his gold Rolex as if time is running out, then looks back at Zoe and rattles off at her: "After your divorce is final from Noah, you're gonna marry me. I'll be richer than original sin itself when my resort is completed. Bank on that, girl. Big will have you farting through silk panties for the rest of your gorgeous life."

Zoe plants her elbows on the bar in front of Big; she leans her chin into her cupped hands and defiantly nails Big's blue eyes with her own big blue eyes. "Everyone knows your Neptune Bay Resort is illegal. You bulldozed tidal lands before the environmental study came in. The ecologists stopped you. You'll be lucky if they don't hang you from an endangered gumbo-limbo tree before you make your first dime."

Hard Puppy snorts his approval of Zoe's put-down of Big. His platinum-encased teeth shine as he speaks with a singsong Caribbean twang. "Baby doll, you don't have to be marryin' me for my monies. Just be givin' me one hot honey night and we be doin' the nasty black and white, then Hard's fortune be yours."

Zoe spins around from Hard and Big. Her attention goes to a large television behind the bar. On the screen, a basketball game cuts away to a breaking news story. A headline scrolls across the screen, MURDER AT THE RACE, followed by a video shot from a helicopter of a race-marker buoy floating at sea. Tied to the pole of the buoy is the blurred image of a man's body. Everyone in the bar stops talking and turns toward the television just as the blurred image of the dead body flashes off the screen and is replaced with DANDY RANDY FOUND DEAD. WE RESUME REGULAR BROADCAST.

Big jumps from his stool and jabs his finger at the television. "That was my Neptune Bay partner tied to that buoy! What the hell happened?"

Hard sneers. "Randy be gone, good riddance. He grew up on this island sellin' bad fish to navy wives. In the end he be tryin' to sell overpriced resort condos to retired military and New York divorcées. Fuck that. His white ass be fish bait now."

Big swings around with doubled-up fists. He takes aim to punch out Hard's mouthful of metallic teeth as a wiry woman, Pat, steps in front of him. Pat wears rubber shrimper boots, blue jeans, and a tight T-shirt. She pulls up onto the stool vacated by Big. Wrapped around the bare skin of her left arm are purple tattooed tentacles of a one-eyed octopus. She nails Hard with a mocking smirk. "Don't be mean about dearly departed Dandy Randy. Show him some respect. That's not any way to talk about your brother."

Hard spews out a mouthful of foaming spit. "Dandy don't be my brother! Dandy be a white cracker boy. My mama never let no rooster wearin' white socks in her back door. No white chickens be in her yard."

Pat laughs at Hard. "Your mama should've ate whatever rooster was your daddy for giving her a big load of crap like you to haul."

Zoe pops open a bottle of beer and slides it across the bar counter. "Here you go, Pat, this one's on the house. Let's keep the peace."

Pat grabs the bottle and swigs the beer. She smacks the bottle back down and stares at Hard.

Hard's angry glare turns into a smile of glinting teeth. "Pat, you be a mean son-of-a-bitch. You should quit shrimpin' and come workin' for me. I could use a scrapper like you."

Pat swipes beer from her sun-hardened lips. "You want me to give up being captain of my own shrimping boat to rig dogfights for you?"

"I be no dogfight gamer. That be a white-devil lie. I be a peaceful man, not like you. Word is you be the number-one killer of leatherback turtles in the Florida Keys."

"Yeah, Chinese dudes pay a fortune for leatherbacks. They believe leatherbacks can cure everything from cancer to limp dick."

Hard smirks. "Who you be accusin' of limp dick? Nothin' between your legs but eight inches of strap-on stiff rubber."

Zoe leans in between Pat and Hard. She beams Pat a friendly heads-up. "Honey, you should use turtle excluders on your shrimp nets. If you're caught slaughtering endangered turtles, they'll lock you up and throw the key away."

Pat shakes her head defiantly from side to side. "I got a right to fish anything from the sea. No one can stop me. No feds, no man, no woman. Not even a woman as sexy as you, Zoe, Miss Show My Cute White Ass in Shorts to All the Customers When I'm Bending Over to Get the Beer."

Big Conch's eyes go to the television, where the basketball players on the screen are replaced by the image of Luz being interviewed by a reporter. Behind Luz is the Haitian raft filled with dead bodies. Big shouts at Zoe. "Turn the goddamned TV up, for Christ's sakes!"

Zoe raises the volume. Luz's steady professional voice fills the room: "They died from hunger and exposure. No indication of foul play. Just a horrendous end for desperate people."

Pat whistles and calls out to Luz on the screen. "Look at you! You're a gorgeous star. They should put you in a Hollywood movie. You could be the warden in a woman's prison."

Zoe pushes a firm finger against Pat's lips. "Quiet. Let's hear what Luz is saying."

Hard bangs his beer bottle on the counter. "Luz be one black sister can't be trusted. I hate cops, 'specially colored cops. Be bad for business."

The outside door to the bar slams open. In the doorway is Hogfish, backlit by a shaft of sunlight. His iPhone earbuds are clamped into his ears. He looks wild-eyed from beneath his long-billed fisherman's cap and screams in panic: "This world is rigged for hurricanes! El Finito's coming! I see the eye of his category-five hurricane winking offshore! Monster of destruction blowing two-hundred-mile-an-hour winds and pushing a fifty-foot-high storm surge before it! I'm the best fishing guide on this island, I read the weather. The ocean's currents spell out the future to me! I see the ocean's truth with my own eyes!"

Big stomps his feet on the floor and shouts back at Hogfish. "You're no fishing guide anymore! You can't find your own pecker to take a piss, let alone find yourself a fish to hook." Big grabs his beer bottle and hurls it at Hogfish.

The bottle flies by Hogfish's head, hitting the wall behind in a shatter of spraying glass. He ignores the shards around him, his head bobbing to music pumping through the earbuds. He lurches violently, seemingly caught by a great wind. He staggers, regains his footing, stands alone in the center of the room, with everyone fixed on his screaming rant.

"Like the baby Jesus grown into a righteous monster, El Finito will shut your mouths and open your minds! You don't need satellite photos to see him coming! Finito is speeding here to punch your lights out! Punch your teeth down your throat! Punch your civilization down the drain!"

A long one of the many deep-water canals running in from the Gulf of Mexico side of Key West and crisscrossing the island stands Noah's nautical-deco-style house. The 1930s structure is long past its glory days, the paint of its once-sleek exterior spider-cracked and peeling. In the hazy humid atmosphere of the setting sun, the rounded walls and porthole windows give the appearance of a formerly glamorous yacht now forsaken and stranded on land.

Inside the sparse living room, a few pieces of worn-out dull-yellow bamboo furniture are scattered around, and piles of dusty hardcover law books and tattered paperbacks are stacked along the walls. Noah sits at a lone bamboo table, listening to the chorus of frogs outside croaking anxiously for night to fall. He takes a drink from his rum bottle and stares pensively through the open window, across a parched grassy expanse, at the still water of the canal. A fish leaps from the flat surface. It snaps into its gaping mouth an unlucky flying insect, then splashes from sight back into the depths of the canal.

Behind Noah, in the rose glow of dusk, Zoe quietly walks in. She sits across from him at the table and watches him drink. The sound of frogs outside grows more insistent, at odds with the measured tone of Zoe's words: "I need you to sign the divorce papers in two weeks. Don't play any tricks."

A nervous twitch crosses Noah's face. He takes another drink. He holds the liquor in his mouth, feeling its sting before swallowing. His throat is tight as his words come out with a cut: "What's the hurry? We haven't been living together for a year."

"You haven't been living for a year."

"Depends on what you call living."

"You're either drunk or out there on your boat, ranting on the radio."

"I'm not an alcoholic. If a man drinks himself into oblivion, it means he doesn't want to see the sun rise the next morning. I still want to see the sun rise."

"You haven't obliterated yourself—yet—but you've given up. You used to be a damn fine lawyer."

"I didn't give up, sweetheart. I was disbarred."

"What did you expect? You went ballistic in the courtroom."

"I was prosecuting corporate bastards drilling illegal wells in protected tidelands. Toxic sludge killing off wildlife. Politicians paid off. Nobody had the guts to stand up against them. Masters and slaves, same as it ever was. At least one day, in one courtroom, before the judge let the criminals off, I could expose them. You know what I always say: speaking the truth will set you on fire."

"I know the story by heart."

"Then don't come in here and lecture me, saying I gave up."

"I don't buy into your excuse of indignation. You didn't have to storm out of the courtroom."

"You didn't have to walk out of the marriage."

"I only walked out when you started drowning yourself in a sea of booze."

"A man who does not enter the sea will not be drowned by the sea, right? Don't worry about me—I'm a good swimmer."

"Nobody is that good of a swimmer."

"What do you want me to say, Zoe? The usual muck: 'Hi, I'm Noah, I'm an alcoholic'? Well, this boy won't play that shtick, because it's really a stick with one sharp end and the other end covered in shit. I will stand up and shout: 'I'm Noah and I fucked up and I don't want sympathy, antipathy, hallelujahs, or condemnations. It is what it is, between a man and himself, a void to swim in until it's a win-or-lose.'"

Zoe pulls the bottle from his hand. She slips the gold wedding ring from her finger and drops it into the empty bottle. The ring falls to the glass bottom with a clink. She hands the bottle back to Noah. "Congratulations, now you're married to it."

"And you've finally got what you want: you're free to date the Big Conchs of this world. That's why you still run a bar, so guys like Big can get drunk and hit on you?"

Zoe bites down on her lip, trying to suppress her fury, but she cannot. "That's disgusting. You know good and well that I got into the bar business years ago only to support you through law school. Why do you try to hurt me like this?"

Noah picks up a cork from the tabletop. He pounds the cork tightly into the bottle's neck. He holds the bottle up and shakes it. The gold ring trapped inside rattles. He stares through the glass at the ring. "Haitian rum. There's a prize in each and every bottle." He shifts his intense gaze onto Zoe. "You are still my prize. My dazzling angelfish, my resplendent butterfly fish, my gorgeous queen triggerfish."

Zoe pushes up from the table. "I'm nobody's fish. Stay

here and drown in the drunken sea of self-pity you've created for yourself." She walks out.

Noah does not move; he sits alone in the stillness. Through the open window from outside, the sickly sweet scent of night-blooming jasmine drifts in. The blood in his veins hums with the sugar rush of rum. On a moisture-slick wall, he watches a gecko make its slow, paranoid way until it senses him watching. The gecko's ghostly-pale color flushes to a bright bold green; the blow bulge under its chin balloons into pulsating crimson. It pumps up on its short legs and puffs its three-inch lizard body into what it thinks is an intimidating size that will back Noah down from any hostile intentions.

Noah raises the empty rum bottle with the ring in it and salutes the gecko. "That's right, buddy, you're the man. You are the man. Don't ever forget it."

Eighteen miles up from Key West, on distant Sugarloaf Key, an eighty-foot-high pyramid-shaped wooden tower looms at the dead end of a gravel road. The moon's glow reveals that the tower is surrounded by a putrid mangrove swamp of twisted trunks and gnarly branches. From the swamp's brackish green water emerges what appears to be a human skeleton. The skeleton is a person totally encased in a full-body black rubber suit stretched tight and painted with luminescent white skeleton bones. A rubber skull mask covers the face and head. The skeleton rises out of the dark water onto the hard gravel road. A coiled rope is slung over its shoulder. The skeleton peers out from deep black eye sockets to see if anyone is watching. It reaches back down and hefts from the swamp's mud-suck of water a heavy object wrapped and tied in a canvas tarpaulin. The skeleton slowly moves along the road, the gravel crunching beneath its rubber feet as it drags the heavy object behind. The skeleton stops and bends its head back, its skull face staring up to the top of the tower's point.

In the blue light of a full moon, the skeleton continues dragging the object toward the tower.

Sharp morning sunlight glares off the pyramid-shaped wood tower surrounded by mangrove swamp. A tour bus travels on the gravel road leading to the tower. The bus's high black rubber tires kick up a cloud of white dust. The bus rolls to a stop in front of the tower. The side of the bus is painted with bright green words: FLORIDA KEYS ECO-AWARE.

Ecotourists step out of the vehicle with eager purpose. Slung around the necks of the men and women are binoculars and cameras. They wear fashionable shorts and green T-shirts emblazoned with DON'T FOOL WITH MOTHER NATURE. They aim their cameras at the wooden pyramid tower.

The last person out of the bus is a tour guide with a

tight expression of righteousness etched on her youthful face. She motions for the group to gather around her. The tourists snap to attention at her words. "Many years ago, a real-estate tycoon had a grand scheme. He wanted to drain this mangrove swamp and build a city here. But first he had to eradicate the mosquito population that swarms by the billions from this swamp. So the clever developer built this eighty-foot-high wooden tower to house thousands of bats. The plan was that at night the bats would fly out from the tower to eat the mosquitoes. It seemed like a good idea at the time, an army of bats gobbling up bloodthirsty mosquitoes."

The ecotourists groan their disapproval of the developer's scheme.

A thin young man wearing a green silk bandanna tight around his forehead speaks up. "Are the bats still inside? I'd just like to—"

A ruddy-faced Australian cuts off the question with his thick accent. "Hell, mate, if the bats are inside, all the bloody buggers will be hanging upside down asleep. Maybe Count Dracula is in there with them. Spoookyyy."

The thin young man looks nervously at the tower. "That's not funny, dude!"

The guide raises her hand for quiet and continues her story. "The developer's grandiose mosquito-eating scheme didn't work. The bats flew away and never returned. The guy went belly-up, lost all his money, and slunk back to where he came from."

The ecotourists give a congratulatory cheer.

The Australian chimes in. "Bloody hell, that served the greedy grubber right."

The guide looks out across the surrounding fetid mangrove swamp of tangled tree trunks and branches. "The Florida Keys are a one-of-a-kind unique and fragile environment which we all must respect and protect. What is the lesson that I've been teaching you on this tour?"

The ecotourists chant in unison: "Don't fool with Mother Nature or Mother Nature will fool with you!"

The guide beams her approval. "Let this tower stand as a living lesson to all those who want to come to our paradise and try to rip it off."

The ecotourists pump their fists, shouting, "Don't fool with Mother Nature!"

"Good. Now, let's take a closer look at this tower and witness one man's folly." The guide leads the group across the crunchy gravel road. She stops beneath the tower's base of massive wooden support struts. She beckons the tourists to gather around. "At one time this was the highest structure in the Florida Keys between Miami and Key West. The tower could be seen by passing ships from miles out at sea. Take a look up and see how high this is—quite a feat."

The ecotourists bend their heads back and look up inside the soaring shaft. In a stunned moment of silence, their eyes widen as they are transfixed by the vision they see in the clammy darkness far above, at the tower's point. Their sudden shouts and screams echo up the shaft in panicked horror. They turn and run between the tower's massive support struts and back onto the road. They attempt to knock one another out of the way as they scramble toward the bus. The thin man with the tight green bandanna is pushed aside and falls onto the road; the gravel cuts into his knees, drawing blood. The tour guide yanks him up by the arm. He looks back toward the tower and his body shakes violently. A spray of vomit shoots from his mouth and splatters at the tour guide's feet. The guide tightens her grip on the wobbling man's arm and runs with him toward the bus, where the others are cowering in their seats.

Luz steers her white Dodge Charger down the skinny slot of Olivia Street. The street is crowded on both sides with century-old Cuban cigar-makers' shacks, built when Key West was the cigar-producing capital of the world, rolling out a million smokes a year. None of the shacks retain their original bare-board anonymity, having been painted by affluent new owners to a pastel prettiness. Gone are the generations of Cubans who once stood on the porches calling out hot gossip to neighbors in hot weather. The humid air no longer carries the garlic scent of sizzling shrimp and the sweet aroma of Cuban bread. The white fences in front of the shacks have been trimmed of their overgrown red bougainvillea and riotous yellow allamanda blossoms. Everything is prim and calm, like a street in a proper New England port town, not the boisterous place where Luz grew up.

Luz turns her car at the corner of Olivia onto wide Duval Street. She parks in front of one of the last Cuban expresso-*buche* shops on the island not retrofitted into a trendy franchise coffee palace. The shop is a nondescript narrow storefront with a slotted hole cut in a cement wall to pass the coffee through. Luz gets out of her car and orders her third *buche* double of the morning. She watches through the slotted hole as a broad-butted Cuban woman dressed in tight blue jeans works at the sputtering and hissing nozzle of a monstrous old burnished expresso machine. The woman turns with a triumphant smile and presents a cup of steaming *buche* to Luz, who cradles it in her hand.

Sipping her hot caffeine nectar in the sun's morning glare, Luz keeps her eyes on the Duval Street activity from behind her sunglasses. Packs of excited vacationers in shorts and flip-flops hurry by on the sidewalk, darting into gift shops, trying on T-shirts with tropical scenes silk-screened on them, and buying Key West's two most famous postcard photos, the mile-zero sign at the end of Highway 1, and the tall bullet-shaped concrete monument at the Atlantic's edge declaring SOUTHERNMOST POINT CONTINENTAL U.S.A.—90 MILES TO CUBA.

From the open window of Luz's car, parked at the curb, a police dispatcher's radio voice drones. Luz takes another sip of *buche* as she listens to the bored voice announcing bicycle thefts, lost dogs, and jaywalkers. The voice is suddenly drowned out by the roar of a motorcycle. She turns to see Pat on her Harley-D jump the curb behind the Charger and come to a tire-burning stop on the sidewalk, scattering the startled tourists.

Luz eyes Pat with mock discipline. "I could arrest you for that stunt."

Pat tightens her grip on the Harley's chrome handlebars. She fixes Luz with a bold stare. "Oh, I want to be arrested. That's my dream, one night locked up with you. I'll lick all the brown sugar out of your bowl. You should jilt your girlfriend, Joan. Hop on my bike. We'll never look back."

Luz swallows her coffee. "You still poaching endangered turtles?"

Pat flexes the muscles of her bare arm with the octopus tattoo, bulking up the one-eyed creature's nasty-looking tentacles. "No one will ever catch me. But, hey, you can catch that ecofreak brother of Joan's. He's broadcasting illegally over the radio."

"Noah broadcasts from outside the city limits. I don't have jurisdiction on the ocean. That's for the feds."

"I hope his pissy pirate boat sinks in the middle of a shit slick dumped from a thousand crappers off a cruise ship."

Pat gazes over at the gleaming white Charger SRT8, taking in its arched rear-end cobra-wing spoiler and the black front grille open-jawed like an onrushing land shark.

She grins. "You got yourself some unmarked cop car, tricked out like a Cuban Miami pimp-mobile. I know there's a siren embedded in that grille, and red strobe-lights under those halogen headbeams that you can switch on from inside. How come you got all the flash, when most of Key West's dumb-dicks poke around in stupid Ford Victorias?"

Luz grins back. "I have this rocket because I'll need it to go a quarter of a mile in twelve seconds when I'm coming to bust your ass."

"Like I said, no one can catch me."

Luz shakes her head and looks long at Pat. *"No hay rosas sin espinas."*

"Huh? I don't *habla* the Es-span-yolla. What are you saying?"

"There are no roses without thorns."

Pat twists her Harley's throttle in a rev and shouts above the engine's loud growl, "I'll take that as a compliment. Whenever you get tired of your blond bunny, you come running to me. I'm the only real rose in the garden. With me you get the prick of the thorns and not just the flower's soft petal. Life on the edge. It's your choice, brown sugar." Pat roars off.

From Luz's police radio, the droning dispatcher's voice suddenly crackles with urgency. "Code five at Sugarloaf Key Bat Tower! All Alpha units respond!"

Luz gulps her coffee and starts her car. She switches on her outside flashing red lights and siren and speeds away.

Luz skids to a stop in front of the pyramid-shaped bat tower. Behind her, Deputy Detective Moxel pulls up in his late-model Ford Victoria police car. They both cut their engines and jump out.

Moxel cocks a hand above his eyes to block the sunlight glaring off the tower as he surveys the situation. He puts on his sunglasses. "I don't see anything going on—place is deserted. Why'd they radio an urgent homicide dispatch? We're even out of Key West jurisdiction up here."

Luz doesn't answer; she hurries toward the tower. Moxel follows with a scowl. They both step under the massive wooden support struts of the tower's broad base.

Luz looks up into the shadowy interior of the ascending wooden shaft and points. "There's our customer."

Moxel pushes in close to Luz and stares up. At the top of the pyramid's narrowing peak hangs a human body. He grabs Luz's arm and pulls her away. "Let's get out of here and call for backup."

Luz shakes loose from Moxel. She grips the first slat of a ladder fixed to the side of the tower. "I'm going up." She starts climbing the ladder, hand over hand, pulling herself into the higher reaches.

Moxel watches Luz climbing farther away and shouts: "You crazy? Could be somebody's baiting a trap with that body. I said we should call for backup."

Luz stops climbing. In the stifling air of the narrow shaft, she wipes sweat from her forehead. She looks back at Moxel below. He seems distant and insignificant. She pulls her pistol out of its holster. She continues climbing into even hotter air. Buzzing flies whiz around her. She waves her pistol at the oncoming flies, and the sudden shift of her body weight puts pressure on the supporting wood slat of the ladder beneath her feet. The slat gives way and tears out with a creaking rip. Luz drops her gun and grabs the slat above her with both hands. She hangs suspended in the air, her legs swinging beneath her. She looks at the slat above that she is hanging on to; the rusty nails securing it begin slowly pulling out.

The sound of Moxel's angry voice rises through the shaft. "Goddamn, I told you to wait. Hold on, I'm coming."

Luz looks down as Moxel makes his way up the ladder. He carefully climbs from one wood slat to the next until he reaches her.

Moxel grabs Luz's dangling legs. "I've got you. Let your weight shift onto me. I'm a strong guy, I'll get you down."

"No. I'm going up."

"You can't. This is a trap. Somebody loosened the nails on these slats to kill anyone trying to get to the body."

"Keep your grip on my legs and push me up so I can grab on to the next slat."

"I can't do that. Our combined weight will rip out the slats and we'll fall."

Luz's brown eyes narrow into severe slits. She speaks in a guttural growl. "That's an order, goddamn it. Boost me up!"

Moxel tightens his hold around Luz's legs. "Okay, but you're going to kill us both." He grunts and boosts her.

Luz grabs on to the next slat, pulling the weight of her body higher until she is able to gain a foothold on the lower slat.

Moxel calls after her, "You don't have a gun."

Luz looks back down. "Stay where you are and keep me covered."

Moxel pulls his gun from its holster and aims it up.

Luz keeps climbing until she reaches just below the pointed peak of the tower; she stops. She tries not to inhale the overwhelming stench suddenly engulfing her. From the crossbeam rafter above swings the naked body of a man hung by a rope noosed around his neck. The man's face is a puffed-up purple blotch. Slimy maggots worm out from the orbs of his chalk-white eyes. His ears have been cut off. His pale lips are sewn shut with fishing line. The pallid skin of his body is spotted with green flies sucking at caked flecks of blood. A steel spear is pierced through the man's chest and out his back. A red **X** is slashed on the skin of his stomach.

T hick brown hard roots of towering Spanish laurel trees heave up the sidewalk ahead of Noah in an uneven roll of cracked cement. The sidewalk glimmers in the morning mist coming in from the sea. He follows the sidewalk with the deliberate movements of a rum-soaked man overcompensating for his off-balance gait, as if he was on an invisible surfboard riding a serpentine wave. Ahead of him, the massive leathery trunk of another Spanish laurel has not only cracked the sidewalk but completely lifted and shattered the cement-covered ground in its mighty thrust skyward, throwing dark limbs out to block the sun. From the tree's overhead branches, tendrils of airborne roots cascade back to earth, forming a roped curtain that swings in front of Noah. He pushes through the dripping curtain of vegetation. A three-story tropical mansion of imposing white clapboard comes into view. The mansion is the last of the many that were built in the nineteenth century, when the island was the wealthiest place in America, a bustling port for merchant clipper ships. The ships, loaded with silk, gold, lace, and pewter, had sailed down the Florida Strait, then hugged the narrow channel along the jagged reef and put into Key West's safe harbor at the mouth of the Gulf of

Mexico. The mansion, built by a mercantile-marine millionaire, has been battered and besieged by storms, its wood shutters slammed and splintered by high winds. The elaborately carved spindles of the second-story balcony circling the exterior have been shrunk by the sun and snapped in half. The tin-stamped roofs of the cupolas rising above the second story on all four corners are rusted through; past rains have entered and begun the process of a rotting collapse.

Noah weaves up to the front of the decaying structure through a spectacular riot of overgrown exotic fauna. At the entrance stand two tall faux-Roman columns, their white plaster surfaces crumbling and chipped. He walks between the columns, pushing through more entangled vines onto a dilapidated, termite-decimated porch. The stained-glass fanlight window above the weather-beaten mahogany door is spider-webbed with cracks, threatening to shatter and crash down. The door is slightly ajar. Noah pushes it open and enters a cavernous foyer. He is surrounded by overstuffed chairs and sofas shrouded in musty dust-covered sheets. From the center of the room, a circular staircase ascends, its lustrous pecan-wood steps now buffed to a dusty dung color. He climbs the rickety staircase, which is only one loose board away from collapsing.

At the top of the staircase, Noah stops and waits for a moment, then walks down a long hallway lined by dark cypress wood. At the end of the hallway, tall arched windows are open to the sea. He looks through an open doorway into a bedroom. He sees Lareck, a once-formidable and celebrated painter now ancient and, like his mansion, barely resembling past glories. Lareck reclines in his pajamas on top of the rumpled sheets of a bed, a large sketchpad propped up on his knees. He dips a brush into the open box of watercolors next to him and paints in quick, intuitive flourishes on the pad.

Facing Lareck, from across the room in front of an expansive bay window, is Zoe, caught by a shaft of vivid sunshine. The light dapples off her high-boned cheeks. She wears a strapless white dress, exposing the tan of her smooth bare shoulders and long legs.

Lareck continues his painting of Zoe as he speaks with a rolling Southern twang; his voice rises and falls in a rush of smoothed-off syllables that nearly become a high-pitched whine. "My dear muse and inspiration, loosen those lips. I don't want you looking like Whistler's sourpuss mother."

Zoe licks her lips, shifts her weight, and moves slightly. "Is this better?"

"That's it. Turn to the right. I want more light on you. Your skin shines with promise. A lifetime of painting, and I still chase the promise."

Zoe turns to a sharper profile angle in the shaft of sunlight. "Like this?" The light fires up her blond hair in a golden halo.

Lareck pushes up on his bed pillows for a better view. "Perfect. You're a pensive Botticelli Madonna gazing out over the Arno River in Florence. You have, my dear, the dreamy gleam of the sassy saints that the Renaissance boys fell over each other trying to capture."

He bends his head toward the pad and paints furiously with aggressive strokes. He puts the brush down, overcome by his creation. He takes a deep breath and sighs, rubs his eyes, and looks around. He glimpses Noah standing outside the open door in the hallway. His voice mellows in a warm greeting. "Noah, come in and sit with me."

Noah enters and sits in a wicker chair with chipped white paint. He is mesmerized by Zoe illuminated in tropical light streaming through the window. She shifts her body nervously at being so close to him. He looks back at Lareck. "Sorry to interrupt. I forgot you have your painting session with Zoe on Wednesday afternoons."

Lareck nods, picks up his brush, and continues his strokes on the large pad. "She's the beautiful daughter I never had. But I've got to paint fast—beauty doesn't last forever."

Zoe gives Lareck a pert, ironic smile. "And you aren't lasting forever. So hurry up, this is a hard pose to hold. I'm getting a muscle pull in my left calf."

Noah looks back at Zoe. "As a poet said, nothing lasts forever, not beauty, not marriage, not even eternal love. But I'm still holding out for you on the eternal love part."

Zoe snaps at him, "Your philosophy comes straight from the bottom of a rum bottle. Too simple, too sugary."

Lareck huffs. "Quiet, your marital bliss is distracting me."

Noah and Zoe stay silent as Lareck continues his strokes on the pad. From the outside hallway, the sound of approaching footsteps is heard. Hogfish appears in the doorway. He steps into the room, bobbing back and forth manically to the musical beat blasting through his earbuds.

A look of dismay spreads across Lareck's wrinkled face. "Ah, my son pops up out of nowhere." Hogfish doesn't hear the words, bobbing agitatedly to his music. Lareck rolls his eyes at Noah and Zoe. "What can I say? Only that a man sends his sperm into a woman's womb like a blind ambassador hoping to make a good deal—but a man never knows what's going to emerge from that womb. It could be a president or a jackass."

Hogfish screams at Lareck: "Pop! You can't stay here! El Finito's coming! His hurricane wind is going to blow right through this window to get you! Run!"

Lareck sighs. "What a cross I must bear. Where I sought the complexities of art, my son sought the simplicity of war. He thought that war was nothing more than a video game played in foreign countries with tanks and guns."

Noah keeps his eyes on Hogfish. "Some men fight for their truth with paintbrushes or pens. Other men fight with bullets and bombs."

Lareck points the sharp end of his paintbrush at Hogfish. "What's necessary about war? The army medics rebuilt my boy's skull with titanium plates and sent him home. Now he's somebody I don't know, convinced a hurricane is coming to wipe us out. I don't know if he hears music through those damn things stuck in his ears or if he's getting instructions from space aliens."

Zoe walks to Hogfish in the center of the room. She stops before him and pulls out his earbuds. His eyes widen with apprehension at her close body. He shudders and stiffens. She stares into his eyes, speaking in a firm voice: "Hogfish, you've survived a personal hell most people can't even imagine. I want you to know, I believe all of your fears are justified."

Hogfish jams the earbuds back into his ears, wraps his arms around himself, and bobs violently.

Luz is ushered into the bright fluorescent-lighted autopsy room of the police morgue by a white-coated lab technician. She nods hello to the Police Chief and Moxel, standing next to a high-wheeled gurney. On the gurney's aluminum surface is laid out the naked dead body of the man Luz found hanging in the bat tower. His skin is a waxy parchment-yellow; the sides of his head are dark gashes where his ears have been slashed off. A gaping purple hollow is in his chest, where the steel arrow was extracted. His lips are riddled with puncture holes from having his mouth sewn shut with fishing line. Luz shakes her head at the brutal sight. "Poor Bill Warren."

The Chief holds up a micro–digital recorder. "One like this was found inside Warren's mouth. The reason his lips were sewn shut was to hold it in. I sent that recorder to Miami for further forensics." He sets the recorder on the gurney, next to Warren's head. "You're going to hear an exact duplicate of the original recording."

The Chief presses the play button on the recorder. From the speaker, a stream of static rises, as if emanating from a deep void and traveling a great distance. Out of the static explodes an electronically altered violent voice in a scathing wail:

"My heart is a ticking bomb waiting to explode.
Your evil will bleed in the streets.
I am a suit of bones,

a vengeful skeleton stalking your island.
I discover wrongdoers bent by corruption and profit.
I am a stab in your conscience,
a knife at your throat,
an arrow in your chest.
My blood-red X of vengeance cannot be escaped.
Boogie till you bounce,
bop till you drop.
I am Bizango."

The raging voice stops. Static noise vibrates the air.

Moxel shifts uneasily. He tries to hide his unease with a sneer of bravado as he peers down at Warren. "Now we have two of Neptune Bay's three partners chopped up like they were attacked by a blind sushi chef. Shit-in-your-pants bizarro stuff."

The Chief clicks off the recorder. "Bizango? It took me a while to recall this monster's strange name. Back in the 1980s, when Luz's father was head homicide detective here, he shot dead a man who called himself by that name. It was a big sensation. You remember that, Luz? When your father killed Bizango?"

"I was just a kid when that happened, so I didn't know much about it at the time." Luz takes a deep breath. "Later I was told the story. Bizango was a serial killer, thought of himself as some kind of righteous assassin. My dad tracked him to where he was hiding and shot him. Bizango had terrified the island. No one knew who he was, because he always dressed in a full-body rubber skeleton suit."

"If this Bizango was shot dead years ago, who the hell is calling himself Bizango now?"

"My dad always said, an evil thing never dies."

Moxel spits out a mocking laugh. "That's mumbo-jumbo, like out of some weird old zombie movie."

Luz stares down at the mutilated body on the gurney. "Bill Warren isn't out of an old zombie movie. He's lying here dead, right before our eyes. We have to deal with it."

The Chief looks quizzically at Luz. "What kind of name is Bizango? You're the one on the detective squad who would know that kind of thing."

"You mean I'd know because I'm the only one who has African blood?"

"Don't play your race card on me. Besides, you're only half black."

Moxel gives Luz a snarky up-and-down look. "Why don't you try playing your gender card instead of your race card? What gender are you, anyway?"

Luz ignores Moxel and answers the Chief. "Bizango is a voodoo avenger; he kills people he regards as traitors. Dad told me that. I don't know more, because voodoo is Haitian and I'm Cuban. We don't practice voodoo—we practice Santería, which is different."

"What did your father mean by traitors? Traitors of what?"

"I don't know. After Bizango was killed, Dad was diagnosed with stage-four lung cancer. Bizango was the furthest thing from his thoughts in those last days." Luz stares at the hole in Warren's chest. "Any information on the arrow he was shot with?"

"Same kind that was shot through the chest of Randy Dandy, but it's not an arrow. It's a steel spear shot from a Pelletier speargun that fires off on a CO_2 cartridge with enough force to take down a great white shark. Pelletier is mostly used by military, banned for sport fishing because the fish don't stand a chance."

Moxel hoots with enthusiasm. "The Pelletier is awesome! I saw it in a cool James Bond movie. Bond used the speargun in an underwater duel with this other dude. Both of them were in dive gear. Righteous battle. What was the name of that movie? It had that blond chick in it whose boobs kept popping out of her swimsuit."

Luz turns her gaze on the red **X** slashed across the pallid skin of Warren's stomach. "Why didn't they clean Bill up? That's the least they could have done, wash the bloody *X* off of him."

The Chief looks at the **X**. "Evidence, Luz. They're still analyzing that *X*. It's not blood."

Moxel butts in. "What is it?"

"Spray paint. Common spray paint." The Chief shrugs. "Our new Bizango is also a graffiti artist. Maybe he's only a guy who thinks he's Andy Warhol and is looking for his fifteen minutes of fame."

Moxel hitches up his gun belt, ready for action. "Who's this Andy Warhol? Let's go get him!"

Floating far offshore between Key West and Cuba in his pirate-radio boat, Noah contemplates the microphone and bottle of rum on the console table before him. He swivels in his chair close to the microphone, then backs off. He picks up the bottle and takes a long slug. As the liquor burns in his throat, he looks out through the saltwater-streaked window. The vast blue ocean surrounds him. He could be the only man alive at the dawn of creation, or the only man alive at the end of the world. He leans in close to the microphone and finds his voice.

"We are in the American tropic, in a zone of constant life, death, birth, and decay. As a poet once said, 'Nothing lasts forever, not even eternal love.' So—here is my advice: don't fall in love with a woman, fall in love with a town. A town doesn't expect you to tell it when you're coming home. A town doesn't ask you to stop drinking. Key West is the perfect town to fall in love with. Key West has more bars than churches, schools, grocery stores, and banks put together. You're always welcome in a Key West bar." One of the three cell phones on the table before Noah flashes its red light with an incoming call. He punches up the call. "Go, pilgrim—you're on pirate radio."

A belligerent male voice spews from the big wood loudspeakers that the cell phone is wired to. "Pirate radio, my ass. You're miles offshore, moaning about love instead of talking about what bought-off corporate-controlled commercial radio refuses to talk about."

"You've got a beef, bully boy, sling it at me. Show me the rage."

"I wanna bitch-slap all the bankster bandits and condo cowboys who are destroying the Florida Keys. The worst are those three Neptune Bay partners trying to bulldoze everything natural and put up a wall of condos that will forever block a man's rightful view of his mother ocean."

"Two of the Neptune partners are now dead. Didn't you

hear the news about Bill Warren found hanging in the bat tower?"

"I don't listen to corporate-controlled news radio."

"Well, there's still one partner left, Big Conch. He wants to build in the proposed great-white-heron preserve. It's not a done deal yet. Neptune Bay is coming up for an approval vote."

"Any corrupt government official who votes approval for Neptune Bay should be hung."

"That's it! Show me the rage!"

"Hang 'em high! Let 'em swing by their necks!"

"You know the mantra?"

"Yeah, don't fool with Mother Nature or—"

"—Mother Nature will fool with you!"

"Keep up the fight. Adios, Dog."

"Next caller, go."

A woman's words slur across the airwaves. "Hey, turtle diddler, you're cute when you croon about falling in love with a town. Your hot voice puts a love hex on me. I'm boiling in your turtle soup."

"Are you stoned?"

"Am I phoned? Of course I'm phoned. I've been phoned all day. That's why I phoned you, didn't I? I want to pet your porpoise. I want to hug your dolphin. Can I show you my age?"

"Rage."

"I'll show you better. I'm pulling my panties down right now. See my raging pussy?"

"Mom, I told you never to call me here."

"Mom? I'm not your fuck—"

Noah cuts off the slurring voice. "Stay on point, pilgrims, no games or I'm cutting this broadcast short. I'm waiting for your call. Good, here's a brave soul. You're live."

"Permian extinction. It's sneakin' up on us."

"Welcome back, Nam vet."

"You remember when Hurricane Wilma came through Key West years back?"

"We all do—lots of damage, took forever to recover from it."

"Yeah, but the real damage wasn't what we expected. Wilma didn't hit us head-on with one-hundred-thirty-mile-an-hour winds, didn't smash us with a crashin' forty-foot-high tsunami wave. Wilma blew across the island, ripped off roofs, uprooted palm trees, then, poof, she was gone. That night, people sleepin' in their beds dreamed that their dog was lickin' their face and wouldn't quit, or they dreamed they were pissin' and couldn't stop. People woke up with water risin' all around them, water risin' up out of the floors of their houses, floodin' the streets, coverin' the cars. It was Wilma's sea surge from under the coral rock of the island inundatin' everything. Like the Old Testament deluge, water just kept risin' with nothin' to stop it. There was panic, everyone was gonna be drowned. Key West was gonna be submerged forever, like Atlantis. Then the water stopped risin'. That was Wilma's sneaky punch. The Permian Extinction Event will be like that. The next mega-explosion will come when least expected, annihilate us all."

"Maybe that's not such a bad thing. Mother Nature takes us out before we pollute the whole damn galaxy."

Noah patches in another call. A brusque male voice bellows. "This is Big Conch, CEO of Neptune Bay Resort."

"Ah, the guy who hits on my wife all the time when he isn't busy raping the environment."

"Don't give me that stink load about the environment. I create jobs. What do you create? *Nada!* You want the Florida Keys turned back into a mosquito-infected mangrove swamp."

"I'd rather live with mosquito bites on my ass than be imprisoned on a concrete island of condos surrounded by a dead sea."

"You're just a dipshit bobbing alone on the ocean, trying to get people to jerk off to phony environmental rage. The truth is, it's all about your wife. She left you. You're a pirate without a treasure."

Noah punches Big Conch off the line. "Fun and games are over for today. Here's something for my lost treasure out there, if she's listening." He picks up a CD. "This is a lament of love lost, sung by a man who has crawled on hands and knees over a thousand miles of broken-glass heartbreak road. Enjoy!"

Noah pushes the disc into the CD player and swivels around in his chair as the song begins. Behind him is the Haitian teenager Rimbaud Mesrine, who has been silently watching the whole time. Noah speaks in French to the boy. "You don't understand anything that's been said here today, do you?" Rimbaud shakes his head. Noah continues: "How old are you, kid?"

Rimbaud answers hesitantly in French. "Sixteen."

"Then you're old enough to understand this." Noah cranks up the volume on the CD player.

The man singing his lament from the speakers slits open the heart of the song with a howl of pain.

High-noon sun slams down on a junkyard of abandoned boats of all types and sizes rotting in brutal tropical heat. Some boats are tilted on their sides; some are mounted on concrete blocks with weeds growing up around them; others have their once-tight wooden hulls snapped open and gaping, like prizefighters with their teeth knocked out. Overhead, in the cloudless washed-out sky, vultures glide in circles, looking down among the junked boats for any sign of a dead opportunity.

Between a row of square-hulled houseboats walks Hard Puppy, dressed in his shiny white silk suit. Hard's white alligator-skin shoes crunch the white coral gravel underfoot as he leads three pit bulls tied to a rope. He stops next to a rusted iron ship anchor half wedged into the ground. He ties the pit bulls to the anchor. He walks back ten feet, swings around, and pulls out a Magnum. He aims the long-barreled gun at the pit bulls straining against the rope. He pulls the Magnum's trigger. A reverberating blast shocks through the air. One of the tied pit bulls drops to the ground with a dying yelp. The two remaining dogs bark and lunge against the new dead weight of the rope restraining them.

The scent of blood and burnt metal fills the air. Hard aims the Magnum and fires again. In front of the two pit bulls, a chunk of dirt is ripped out and tossed up in a dust cloud. Hard shouts at the dogs, "Keep your asses still!" He grips the gun in both hands, aims, and fires. A bullet zings through the air, striking a pit bull between the eyes. The bullet's sudden impact explodes the dog's head in a spew of blood, bone, and flesh.

Behind Hard, a white Dodge Charger roars up and brakes to a stop in the gravel. Luz opens the front door and gets out. Hard swings his Magnum around in his two-handed grip and aims it at Luz. She pushes the bottom of her guayabera shirt aside, exposing her holstered Glock; she steadies her hand on the handle and calls out to Hard across the gravel expanse, "Let's have an even fight. Killing a cop isn't as easy as killing a helpless dog."

Hard's lips curl back, exposing his platinum teeth. "Man's got a right shootin' his own dogs." He grins with a quick lick of his lips and glances over at the last pit bull standing. "I got one more slacker to pop off."

"Target practice is finished. Hand over your gun."

Hard kicks at the gravel with the tip of his alligator shoe. A puff of dust floats up. He shoots Luz a defiant stare.

Luz steps straight up to Hard. "I'm going to run a check on your gun to see the nasty places it's been. Maybe it's left a calling card in places where the sun no longer shines."

Hard grips his Magnum harder. "I ain't worried 'bout no checkin'. My hardware be clean. Better you get your head out of your ass. Get in touch with your half-nigga side. Let this whole thing slide."

"It slides if you cop out on the Dandy Randy and Bill Warren murders."

"Ah, colored girl, don't be a shit-kicker. A shit-kicker sees a big ol' pile of shit on the street and kicks it. Best you pass this Neptune Bay shit by. It could stick to your shoes—worse, stink up your life."

"I'm kicking your shit. I'm taking you in for questioning on the two murders."

"You crazy bitch. This black boy got nothin' to do with offin' white chumps. You should be sniffin' in the direction of Big Conch's white ass. Everybody knows Big's the only Neptune partner left."

"No. Maybe you partnered with Big to launder your dogfight winnings through Neptune Bay. Maybe you and Big didn't want to share that with the other two partners. So, whiff, off go Dandy and Warren."

A sweat breaks out across Hard's forehead. "I ain't scammin' with Big. I be a respectable biz-niz man. That's why I be wearin' a suit in this scaldin' sun. No other black boy as pro-fesh-shu-nal as I be."

"Blood-money gambling on pit bulls tearing each other apart is not a profession, it's a crime. You think you can dodge the law, moving your secret dogfights between Key West and Miami. Someday I'll bust you on it, bust you to pieces."

Hard turns and looks across the gravel at the whimpering pit bull roped to the anchor. Around the dog, the blood from the two sprawled dead animals has leaked out in a damp red circle. Hard raises his Magnum and points it at the whimpering pit bull. "You want that dog?"

"I don't want a fighting dog."

"That dog be no fighter, he be a lover. That's why I poppin' him. He'd rather lick his balls than fight. That's why his name be Chicken. You want Chicken or not?"

Luz studies the pit bull squatting on its haunches in a pool of blood. The dog's pink tongue dangles out as it whimpers; one of its ears is a gnarly stub, bitten off in a fight. The hair of the dog's short black coat is slashed with white scars left over from the vicious bites of past battles.

Hard chuckles. "Take Chicken home to that baldheaded daughter of yours. She could use a friend."

"I'll take the dog."

"Deal."

Hard walks across the gravel. He unties the pit bull from the two dead dogs and leads it back to Luz. The sun glints off of Hard's smiling metallic mouthful of teeth. "Now you finally got a friend for your crippled daughter."

Luz's knee whips up in a powerful jackknife kick straight into Hard's groin. Hard's Magnum flies from his hand. He grabs his groin in an anguished wail, gaping at Luz with eyes wide in shock. She rips her pistol from its holster and smacks the gun's gorilla-grip handle against the side of Hard's head with a loud crack. Hard drops to the ground, his feet kicking out at the gravel in pain. Luz stands above Hard, who is writhing in the dust. She aims her pistol down at him.

"You mention my daughter again, I'll kill you!"

A line of shrimping boats is anchored along a concrete pier jutting out into Key West Harbor. The boats' tall masts and winged outriggers are decorated with strands of twinkling white lights. On the pier, a band plays festive Caribbean music to a crowd of shrimpers, their families, and town locals gathered beneath an overhead banner declaring SHRIMP FLEET BLESSING. In the crowd are Luz and Joan with Carmen and Nina. Nina sits in her wheelchair, her brown eyes taking in the scene with nervous excitement.

Big Conch bullies his way through the center of the crowd. He holds two bottles of beer as he cocks his head back and forth, looking for someone. He spots Zoe dancing with a shrimper, her flared skirt spinning around her bare knees as the delighted partner stomps his white rubber boots to the band's percussive rhythm. Big closes in on the shrimper and shoves him aside. The man stops dancing and sizes up Big's imposing stature. The man slinks off. Big offers Zoe one of his two beers. She turns her back on him.

At the edge of the crowd, Hogfish wheels to a squeaky stop on his rusty bicycle. Stretched between the handlebars is the taut fishing line strung with barbed J-hooks. He jerks his head back and forth to the music he hears through the earbuds jammed into his ears and rises from the bicycle's worn leather seat. He looks over the dancing crowd and glimpses Big following close behind Zoe as she walks quickly away from him.

Out of the darkness behind the line of docked shrimping boats, Noah's trawler motors up. Inside the pilothouse, Noah steers his vessel between two large boats and cuts his engine. He looks through the window at the crowd on the pier. Behind him in the shadows is the slight figure of Rimbaud. Noah turns and speaks reassuringly in French: "Do what I told you and stay out of sight. Don't go out on the deck. I'll return soon."

Rimbaud grabs Noah's arm. "I'm afraid. What if they find me?"

"They won't find you if you stay hidden inside the storage closet."

Rimbaud's eyes widen with fear. "They'll find me and send me back to Haiti, where the earthquake cracked open the underworld, releasing zombies. Zombies breathing the death of cholera search for innocents to suck out their life."

"Trust me, I'll protect you. You won't be sent to Haiti. I'll come back with someone who can help us."

Distrust crosses Rimbaud's face as he slips away toward the storage closet.

Noah heads for the door and steps out of the pilothouse onto the deck. Anchored next to the trawler is a shrimping boat with its name painted along its side, *Pat's Pride.* Pat stands on her deck, dressed in men's jeans, shirt, and white rubber boots. She spots Noah and shouts above the raucous music from the band on the pier: "Truth Dog, we're blessing shrimping boats here! Not pirate-radio boats! Shove off!"

Noah shouts back: "If you swear to stop net-killing endangered turtles, I'll shove off! Until then, you can fuck off!"

Pat turns her back on Noah and bends over. She slaps her blue-jean-covered butt with a loud smack. "Kiss it, sucky eco-boy!"

On the crowded pier, a Catholic priest appears, dressed in a long billowing red robe. The priest is followed by altar boys in starched white cloaks. The boys swing metal censers smoking with burning incense. The crowd falls silent. The band stops playing. All eyes go to the priest. He holds high a gold cross with a nailed Jesus. He looks at the long line of shrimping boats with their decorative lights blinking against the black sky. His voice booms: "Father, our shrimping boats are about to sail out again. We pray thee, Father, fill the nets of our men with thy bountiful gifts. We also beseech your Holy Mother, Mary, to shine her guiding light on our brave men, protect them from danger and stormy seas, return them home to the bosom fold of their families and loved ones." The crowd shouts, "Amen!"

An old white-haired black shrimper walks with halting steps in front of the boats. His face is etched with deep lines from a lifetime under the sun. He holds in his hands a large fluted conch shell. He stops and raises the narrow end of the pink luminescent shell to his lips. He takes a deep breath and blows a high-pitched melancholic note.

Nina, seated in her wheelchair next to Luz, bends her head to the conch shell's unsettling wail. She becomes agitated. Luz places her hands on Nina's shoulders to calm her. The old shrimper blows harder into the shell, forcing a shrill note into the night air. Nina's frail body trembles.

The old shrimper keeps blowing as women from the crowd step to the edge of the pier, facing the anchored boats. The women hold large bunches of long-stemmed white roses. They solemnly toss the flowers at the brightly painted high hulls of the boats. The roses hit the wooden hulls with soft thuds and fall below, where they scatter on the water and float around the boats. Zoe, among the women, tosses all of her roses except her last one, which she keeps, breaking off its long green stem, then securing its prominent white bloom next to her ear.

Noah jumps down from the deck of his trawler onto the pier and walks toward Zoe. He is grabbed roughly from behind. He spins around, staring straight into the face of Hogfish.

Hogfish screams urgently: "Roses can't stop El Finito from coming! Listen to the roses talking! Chattering away like mourning widows of drowned shrimpers! They're saying the Devil's wind is winding up to punch the lights out of civilization! Roses are crying because the hurricane is coming!"

From behind Hogfish, at the far end of the pier, Big Conch lights the fuse of a fireworks cannon-barrel launcher. Shrieking fireworks sail high into the night sky and explode, illuminating the uplifted faces of the cheering crowd.

From inside Noah's trawler, Rimbaud stares wide-eyed through the pilothouse window. His terrified face lights up from fireworks bursting with brilliant streamers. He cringes at the exploding sounds and twists his body in sharp turns, as if each of the flaring fireworks has him as its intended target. He falls to his knees and scrambles, with his head down, from the pilothouse out onto the deck. Fireworks whistle in the air around him; dazzling light showers down from above. He scurries to the boat's edge and hurls himself overboard, plunging from sight beneath the water.

The crowd on the pier watches the last of the trailing light fade from the night sky. A belligerent voice calls out, "Fuck the eco-Gestapo!" The crowd turns to Pat, unfurling a canvas banner from her boat's side railing. The banner proclaims NO TURTLE EXCLUDERS ON SHRIMP NETS! Some in the crowd break into an eruption of cheers at the sight of the banner. Pat shouts defiantly: "Listen, all of you! My family fished turtles for generations off of Key West. No eco-Gestapo can dictate to me. I'll net turtles, harpoon turtles, hook turtles, kill turtles with my bare hands if I want. The ocean is the last free frontier, the final home of the brave."

More cheers burst from the crowd, followed by loud boos from others. Men angrily wave their fists and shove one another, their reddened faces inches apart. Women jostle each other, screaming vulgar insults. The priest frantically waves his gold crucifix in the air, but he is ignored.

The band strikes up a sudden rhythmic dance tune. Noah breaks away from Hogfish and makes his way to Zoe. He slips his arm around her waist and spins her in a dance to the band's beat. Some in the crowd stand back, giving Noah and Zoe room; others join in the dancing. Luz lifts Nina up from the wheelchair and sways her in her arms to the joyous rhythm.

Zoe stops dancing and pushes Noah away. "If I want to dance with you, I'll make the choice." She pulls out the white rose tucked behind her ear and hands it to him. "You didn't know you were in a garden of roses when you had it."

Noah holds the rose up and plucks off a petal. "She loves me." He plucks off another petal with a brave grin. "She loves me not."

"You can pluck every petal off that rose, but it won't bring me back. Marriage is not a one-way street just going your way. The street goes both ways." She turns and walks off, leaving Noah alone with his rose.

Along the entire length of the concrete pier, the diesel engines of shrimping boats roar to life. The crowd rushes to the pier's edge, waving good-bye to the boats motoring away. The lights of the fleet become distant on the sea's horizon.

Long after the fleet has disappeared and the crowd has left the pier, Noah and Luz stand alone in the night in front of Noah's trawler. A stiff breeze off the ocean blows in, tugging at Luz's white guayabera shirt. She looks impatiently at Noah. "It's late; I need to get home to my family. Why did you ask me to stay behind with you?"

"I need your help with something. I didn't want to mention it in front of Joan."

"I don't keep secrets from Joan. What's so important that can't be talked about in front of your sister?"

"I'll show you." Noah leads the way onto his trawler. They walk across the deck into the dark pilothouse. Noah switches on the overhead light and calls out in French, "It's safe! No need to hide!" He waits for an answer— silence—calls out again: "This woman I brought can help." He moves to the storage closet in the corner, pushes back its canvas curtain, and looks inside. "Damn, the boy is gone."

"What boy?" Luz walks to the closet and peers in. "Who's supposed to be in here?"

Noah doesn't answer. He picks up a half-finished bottle of rum from the broadcasting table and uncorks it. He takes a swig as he stares through the pilothouse window at the ocean. "Makes no difference now who he is. He's vanished."

L uz steers her white Charger down the main drag of Duval Street. The flanking sidewalks are crowded with gawking tourists passing gaudy trinket shops, boisterous open-air bars crowded with long-haired motor-cycle bikers, tattoo parlors filled with glassy-eyed stoned teenagers, and chattering people at outdoor restaurant tables beneath towering banyan trees. Luz keeps a vigilant eye for lowlife crack dealers, skinhead punks pimping young runaway girls from the North, and tweaked meth-heads looking to start a fight with someone, or with themselves, or with a plate-glass window.

Sitting next to Luz in the passenger seat is Chicken, the one-eared scarred pit bull. Chicken licks his chops as she takes a deep-fried conch fritter from a bag wedged between her thighs. She munches on the fritter as she continues to drive with one hand on the steering wheel. She glances over at the dog, sitting patiently on his haunches, waiting for a handout. "Chicken, you want a fritter?" The dog whines with pitiful expectation. She plucks a fritter from the bag and holds up the greasy ball to Chicken's mouth. "Careful, don't bite my fingers off." The dog's pink tongue slurps the fritter gently from between her fingers. He swallows with a loud gurgle. She pats his broad head affectionately. "You really are a lover, not a fighter. I like that in a man."

Luz turns off Duval Street and drives out of town, past streets lined with palms shading eighteenth-century wood houses painted in bright Caribbean colors. She continues on to the outskirts of Key West, with its sleazy motels, fast-food drive-in joints, and run-down shopping centers. She heads up the Overseas Highway, crossing bridges linking the islands of the Keys. The farther Luz travels, the less man-made distractions line the highway, until, finally, there are none. On one side are the Gulf of Mexico's turquoise-colored waters. On the other side, the vivid indigo of the Atlantic Ocean. She looks through her car's windshield; the atmosphere is pristine, dominated by the changing light reflected from the two great bodies of water. In the pale-blue sky, spread-winged white herons sail between columns of clouds. The herons soar high on hot wind currents, then swoop down, gliding to graceful landings in a flutter of wings on distant mangrove islands dotted across the horizon.

A large billboard looms up on the side of the highway declaring COMING SOON! NEPTUNE BAY RESORT! The billboard's visual depicts a vast resort of luxury condos, hotels, golf courses, and a yacht marina. Towering above the resort depiction is a giant image of the bearded sea god Neptune clutching a trident spear. Luz turns her car abruptly off the highway onto a dirt road leading into the center of an abandoned construction site stripped of all vegetation and empty of any people. She parks the car and gets out. Chicken follows her as she walks across a scraped-earth landscape dominated by rows of hulking, dust-covered bulldozers, earth-graders, dump trucks, and cement mixers. She continues, zigzagging between incomplete cement building foundations with rusted iron rebar struts sticking up from them. She arrives at a concrete pier jutting out into a brackish backwater inlet coming in from the Gulf of Mexico. She walks to the far end of the pier, where a canary-yellow forty-foot powerboat is tied, its high jet-exhaust chrome spoilers gleaming in the harsh sunlight.

In front of the powerboat, Big Conch sits in an aluminum slingback chair, wearing only a tight red Speedo swimsuit. His sinewy suntan-oiled body is shaved of all hair except for the dyed slick blond hair of his head. On his chest glint heavy antique Spanish medallions that dangle from a gold chain around his neck. He shucks oysters with a broad-bladed knife. Scattered around his bare feet are empty shells. Chicken trots up, sniffs the shells, and starts nibbling on them. Big looks up and greets Luz with a smirk as he nods toward Chicken. "I see they finally gave you a better partner than that Riviera redneck, Moxel. At least this one's got a pair of balls."

Big pulls a gnarly-shelled oyster from a wooden crate next to the aluminum chair. He deftly knifes open the shell and scrapes free its meat. He holds out the glob balanced on the knife's blade. "You want an aphrodisiac from the sea? Neptune's original Viagra. It'll give you a hard-on for that hot blond-bombshell girlfriend of yours. Oh yeah, you can't get a hard-on. What is it you get, anyway, if you can't get a stiff dick? Come on, have an oyster. It might even make me attractive to you."

"I just lost my appetite."

"No appetite from stuffing fritters all day. You won't die from a bullet to your heart but a grease hole through your gut." Big holds the knife up to his mouth. He lets the oyster balanced on the blade slide off between his lips.

Luz looks over at the name emblazoned on the power-boat's sleek hull: *Big Conch.*

She looks back at Big. "Since you know so much about the sea, did you know that if a conch's johnson is bitten off by a hungry eel, the conch grows himself a new johnson?"

"Is that why you eat conch fritters all day, hoping to grow yourself a wiener?" Big glances over at Chicken, crunching a mouthful of oyster shells. "Dumb bastard's gonna puke." He turns back to Luz. "You didn't drive all the way out here to give me a lesson on the sex life of the conch. What the hell do you want?"

"Dandy Randy and Bill Warren were both murdered."

"So were the Kennedy brothers. Ancient news. Get to it. You're here because you figure I killed my two partners."

"No. I'm here because I believe whoever did kill your partners is now after you. You should back off developing this resort and lay low."

"Lay low? Never. I don't give a shit if half the people accuse Neptune Bay of destroying the habitats of every-thing from white herons to blind manatees to one-armed nuns. The other half of the people love me for this hundred-million-dollar resort I'm developing. It means jobs to build it, jobs to sell it, jobs to service it. We're com-ing off the worst economic times in the history of the Keys since the Great Depression, and I'm the man leading the way out with my Neptune Bay."

Chicken bumps up against Big's knees and vomits a gut-load of half-eaten oyster shells onto Big's bare feet. "Get out of here, you one-eared mutt!" Big kicks the dog in the ribs. He shouts at Luz as she pulls the yelping Chicken away: "And don't you come around trying to trick me by pretending you care about saving my hide from some psycho killer. And I damn well don't need lecturing about how conchs grow their dicks, especially since you don't have a dick and balls. Hell, you no longer even have tits. You're a sorry-ass situation."

Luz glares at Big. "You've got balls . . . balls for brains."

"I'm a sympathetic man, so I won't respond to that, but answer me this: why, after your mastectomy, didn't you get some fake titties? You're a good-looking woman. You'd be a knockout if you bolted on a pair of Vegas-showgirl silicon hooters. That way you wouldn't look so much like a . . ."

"Dyke."

"Like a guy trying to be tough but he's a punk."

Luz's eyes narrow. She nods at the thick gold chain glinting around Big's neck. *"Un mono que lleva cadenas de oro es todavía un mono."*

"Speak American."

"A monkey wearing gold chains is still a monkey."

Big roars with laughter. "Fu-fuck . . . ing . . . monkey. That's great. A goddamn fucking monkey." His laughter turns to a snarl as he jumps up and slashes the blade of his knife in the air. "I'm not a fucking monkey, you dumb dyke! I'm a goddamn two-hundred-pound male gorilla with five-pound balls and a swinging foot-long dick! Don't you ever forget it!"

Luz faces Big. "I can see from the tiny bump in that Speedo you're wearing that there isn't much swinging between your legs. You don't have enough juice to knock up a tick."

Luz nervously chews on a conch fritter as she watches the Duval Street night action through the windshield of her parked Charger. She keeps her eyes on the front of a nightclub. A neon rainbow sign arches above the nightclub's doorway: LITTLE ORPHAN TRANNY'S. The sign's garish pastel light reflects on three six-foot-tall drag queens with big hair, wearing sequined ball gowns, sashaying back and forth on the sidewalk on six-inch-high stiletto heels. The queens wink false eyelashes, blow kisses, and call out in basso male voices at passing locals, tourists, and high rollers to enter the nightclub and experience the wild side.

Inside her car, Luz slips another fritter from the paper bag between her legs. Chicken sits beside her, expecting a treat. Luz hands the fritter to Chicken, and he tongues it from her fingers. She continues watching the people going in and out of the nightclub, looking for drug pushers and their clientele of tweaked, cranked, and cracked users and abusers. She flips on her car's AM-FM radio and switches through the channels until she locks into a weak station. She turns up the volume and listens to the animated voices of Noah's broadcast coming in through the static.

"Hey, Truth Dog, I'm a Key West shrimper."

"Welcome, shrimper. You're on pirate radio."

"It pisses me off that so many of your callers are against commercial shrimpers and long-liners here in the Keys.

We're seen as rednecks who don't give a shit about marine ecology. Hell, we're the ones who make a living from the sea. You won't find stronger guardians of marine life than us."

"I'm with you. Many of the old-timers here were the original ecologists, against the slaughter of the turtles, whose meat was being turned into steaks and soup, their shells made into combs and toothbrushes."

"Right, we were the first to use excluders on our boats. We were the first to use safety O-hooks instead of J-hooks on our longlines."

"My rage is against those who refuse to do that. You know how many endangered female leatherback turtles are left laying their eggs in the sands of Florida's east coast?"

"Not many."

"Fewer than two hundred. Down from tens of thousands. Turtles have been around a million years and we're wiping them out. We're snagging, tangling, drowning, hooking the last of the turtles every day with gill nets, drift nets, drag nets, and J-hook longlines."

"And the plastic bags?"

"Don't get me started! Billions of bags dumped into the ocean each year, choking, gagging, and strangling turtles to death!"

"Goddamn shame."

"God had nothing to do with it. Man did it."

Luz cuts off Noah's radio voice, her attention caught through her windshield by a man and a teenaged girl down the street, coming out of the Trouble in Paradise cocktail lounge. The man and girl walk away with their backs to Luz. She blurts out to Chicken, sitting next to her,

"That's my Carmen! She snuck out of the house!" Chicken licks his chops for more fritters.

Luz starts her Charger and steers it onto Duval Street, following behind the man and teenager. The girl's long black hair hangs down to the top of a yellow miniskirt hugging her bottom so tightly that her firm butt cheeks are prominently outlined. The man runs his hand over her butt as she walks.

"I know my own daughter when I see her. I shouldn't have let her paint those damn fingernails. I knew it would lead to no good."

The man and teenager turn suddenly off of Duval Street toward Grunt Bone Alley. Luz presses down on the accelerator pedal and speeds up. A fast-moving line of hooting college kids on loud mopeds shoots out from the alley. Luz honks her horn at the riders blocking her car, but the mopeds keep coming. She spots an opening in the line and guns into Grunt Bone Alley. The narrow lane is deserted except for cars parked along its sides. She pulls over and cuts her engine. She studies the parked cars. Chicken looks at the bag of fritters and whines. She pats Chicken's head. "Shush. They're around here somewhere."

In the dark distance of the lane, there is no movement except from a rusted 1961 Pontiac GTO parked in front of a row of garbage cans. The GTO slightly bounces on its tires. Luz keeps her gaze fixed on it. In the car's back window, a man's head suddenly pops up in silhouette. The head quickly disappears back down.

"He's raping Carmen in the back seat!"

Luz jumps from her car and runs down the alley to the GTO. She yanks open the car's back door and shines her flashlight beam in on a man's bare white ass as his body humps up and down on the teenager beneath him. Luz grabs the man's hair with one hand and jerks his head around. She beams the flashlight into his eyes. "You're under arrest for raping a teenager!"

The surprised man yells, "What the fuck are you talking about?"

"The girl's only sixteen!"

"Like hell! She's eighteen!"

Luz swings her beam at the girl spread-eagled on her back beneath the man. Her long black hair is tangled over her face. Her bare breasts heave from rapid breathing. Her skirt is pushed up and her panties are pulled down. In the dark V between her naked thighs glistens a worm of spilled cum. The teenager shakes the tangled hair away from her face. Luz stares at the face brightly lit in the flashlight beam. The teenager is not Carmen.

The girl glares at Luz. "I can prove I'm eighteen. My driver's license is in my purse."

Luz takes a deep breath. "No, you're not eighteen. I recognize you. You're the Munoz girl. I know your family. I was at your Quince party two years ago. You're just seventeen."

"That was three years ago! I'm eighteen now!"

Luz steps out of the car and looks at the man. "Pull your pants up, you chicken-hawk bastard."

The man gets out of the car. He shoves the still-hard stub of his prick beneath his underpants, hitches up his blue jeans, and winks at Luz. "I bet you wish you could whack off a piece of her yourself. She's not underaged. She's street legal. You can't arrest me. Can't do a fucking thing."

"Don't count on it. I see you with her again, I'll toss you

into lockup, where your new boyfriends will be waiting for your white ass. Get the hell out of here!"

The man takes off running. The teenager climbs out of the car. Luz grabs her wrists and handcuffs her.

"You can't take me prisoner! What are you doing! I didn't do anything wrong!"

Luz stays silent. She marches the teenager to the Charger, shoves her into the back, and slams the door. In the front seat, Chicken turns around and puts his front paws on the seat separating him from the teenager. He cocks his one ear, wanting to lick her hello with his tongue. Luz jumps into the car next to Chicken. She looks into the rearview mirror at the teenager in the back.

The handcuffed girl stares defiantly. "This is illegal. You can't do this. My dad's brother is a big-time lawyer in Miami. Manny Munoz—you ever heard of him? He'll sue you!"

"Let him sue."

"And he'll sue you for having this mangy mutt in a cop car. I bet that's against cop rules. Hey, but this isn't a cop car! What's going on?"

"I'm not a cop. I'm a plainclothes detective."

Luz starts the Charger and drives off. She hears the teenager crying in the back seat. Luz weaves through dark back streets until she arrives before the twelve-foot-high bullet-shaped concrete monument lit up in the car's headlights. Bold black-painted words declare SOUTHERNMOST POINT CONTINENTAL U.S.A.—90 MILES TO CUBA.

Luz drives behind the monument, where the street abruptly ends and the Atlantic Ocean begins. She turns off the car's engine and rolls down her side window. The ocean's surface ahead is a black mirror in the night. A rush of salt-scented air fills the car. She looks in the rear-view mirror at the crying teenager. "You smell that?"

The teenager sniffles. "Please don't tell my parents about my boyfriend. I beg you. He's thirty-two. They'll kill me."

"Take a deep breath. Smell the air."

"It's salty."

"It's the air of Cuba blowing in from across the Florida Strait."

"I beg you not to tell my parents."

"That's the air of your great-grandparents. People who immigrated to Key West in the eighteen hundreds with nothing and built a life. Hardworking people who had pride and morals. People who brought those qualities with them."

"I'll just die if you tell my parents."

"The problem now is, no pride, no morals."

"Listen, lady, we're friends, right? I remember you at my Quince. You were there with your girlfriend."

"Not girlfriend. Life partner. Love of my life."

"Whatever."

Luz turns on the car radio. She switches through the stations, playing rock, country, and Latin music. She stops on the voice of Noah coming in. She glances at the girl in the rearview mirror. "Do you know who this is?"

"Isn't he that pirate guy?"

"Yes."

"Nobody I know cares about him."

"You should care. He's about saving what counts. He's fighting for what good is left in this world for your generation." Luz faces the girl. "Listen to Noah, then I'll let you go."

"You won't tell my parents about what happened?"

"I won't tell them if you learn something here tonight."

Luz turns up the volume on Noah's voice.

The girl slumps in the back corner of the car. Her face turns sullen as Noah's words crackle from the radio.

You've got to work with me tonight, pilgrims, or ol' Truth Dog is going to sail away back home. We've got four endangered turtle species here in the Florida Keys: the leatherback, the loggerhead, the hawksbill, and the green. Why can't we stop the slaughter? I'm waiting for your answer. Okay, here's a pilgrim. Talk me some sense."

A woman's shaky voice answers. "I never called before. I'm so nervous."

"You'll be fine."

"You know, uh, there's been, uh, extensive scientific research into cancer. They've scrutinized Neanderthal fossils and found no evidence of cancer. Cancer only shows up two hundred years ago. It's modern times that have surrounded us with cancer and . . ."

"Don't stop. I'm here for you."

The nervous woman's voice becomes emboldened. "Remember when you said the dumping of toxic stuff by the military around the Keys might have poisoned the water?"

"Military's been here since the Civil War. Ships, submarines, fighter jets, you name it. Toxic dumping is our legacy."

"Now we have abnormally high rates of cancer."

"I always say, you want the true picture, you've got to connect the right dots."

"The picture is," the woman says, sobbing, "everything is being poisoned. People, coral reefs, sea life, everything is going to die of man-made cancer."

"You're right. It's all connected. Next caller, you're up. Connect the dots."

A squeaky male voice begins excitedly: "What's that ditzy dame talking about? She's got cancer on the brain. Everybody wants to cure cancer, but it's the witty bitty we should worry about."

"Witty bitty?"

"The Key Largo cotton mouse. It's on the official endangered list. It's being wiped out by runaway cats from trailer camps." The squeaky voice drops to a confidential tone. "Truth Dog, I'm reaching out my hand to you. Will you pray with me?"

"Whatever floats your boat. Okay."

"You got my hand?"

"I got it. It's sweaty."

"We pray thee, Lord, to keep safe all your creatures great and small. Especially the witty bitty."

"Maybe the Head Man up above will hear your prayer."

"Oh, he will. He's listening right now. He's going to show you the light. Good-bye, brother."

"Next caller. Go. I'm waiting. . . . I said, go."

The baritone of a man's belligerent voice slams through the silence. "I'm the vet who called before."

"Welcome back, vet."

"I saw bad shit in Nam. Shit that makes what happened in Iraq and Afghanistan look like a Disneyland ride. A famous photo was taken durin' the Nam war. It showed a naked Vietnamese girl runnin' up the road. Her village had been napalm-flamed by us. She was on fire. Blobs of smolderin' napalm burnin' off her skin. That stricken look on her face—fuck, man—that look! That was the look of innocence destroyed by our evil."

"That's it, show me the rage."

"I was one of the guys napalming those Nam villages. I was nineteen years old. I still see that girl's smolderin' skin in my dreams, nearly half a century later. The smell of burnin' flesh wakes me up every night."

"The smell of rage."

"I saw the same look that girl had in another photo more recently, when that oil well blew in the Gulf."

"Deepwater Horizon blowout. Worst ecological disaster in American history. Total cover-up."

"It was a photo of a pelican flounderin' in a sea of oil. The bird's body was drenched in brown slime, its wings stretched out, tryin' to fly, but it couldn't. Its eyes were huge with fear, like that girl's eyes, that girl with her skin on fire runnin' up the road. We've got to stand against innocents' being slaughtered."

"We've got to stand up to the war machine that runs on soul-sucking oil or our days are numbered."

"That's why I called before about the comin' Permian Extinction Event. Next time I'll call with proof that it's all gonna blow sky-high."

Seagulls swarm in the sky above Pat's shrimping boat as it plows through heavy ocean swells far out at sea. The boat's long-poled twenty-foot outriggers are winged out on both sides of the vessel, their unfurled dragnets roiling the water. Pat swings in one of the outriggers and cranks up its dripping net. The net breaks the surface of the water, weighted with a squirming catch of pink-shelled shrimp. Pat pulls the rip cord on the net as it swoops in over the deck. A small catch of briny shrimp drops from the net onto the deck. She yanks off her canvas captain's cap and whacks it in frustration against her blue jeans. She whips around to her boat mate, standing next to her. The mate is shirtless, the sun-darkened skin of his broad upper torso swirled with wicked-looking interlocking tattoos. He hikes his tight jeans up and takes a boxer's stance in his white rubber shrimper boots, expecting a punch from frustrated Pat as she shouts: "We've been out here for three days, and all I get is a twenty-buck load of pink bug-eyes! I can't even pay my fuel with that!"

The mate cocks a hand over his eyes and squints at the sunlight's glare on the ocean. "Looks like your luck is taking a turn." He points to a bubbling break on the water's surface. A pod of fast-moving dolphins leaps from the water into the air, their bodies twisting in muscular turns as they approach the side of the boat.

Pat claps her hands together. "Hallelujah, let's get some bait for the longlines!" She runs into the pilothouse and races back out with a shotgun. She takes a position on the prow of the boat as the pod of dolphins nose-dive back beneath the water and disappear. She aims the shotgun at a calm spot in the water in front of the boat. She waits. The dolphins break through the surface of the calm spot in a gushing spray of saltwater; sunlight shimmers on their sleek, wet bodies arched high in the air. She fires a blast from the shotgun. Blood spews from one of the arched dolphins. The others dive from sight, leaving the dolphin with its side blown open floating on the sea close to the boat. Pat puts down the shotgun, grabs a long gaffing pole, and whams its steel hook-point into the floating dolphin. The mate short-gaffs the creature from the other side. Together they heft the dead weight up onto the deck.

Pat grins with delight at the mate. "Hurry, get that bucket of J-hooks." She pulls out her knife from the leather holster belt strapped around her waist. She grips the knife and slashes at the dolphin's thick dorsal fin, curved up high from the center of its back. The blade cuts through the fibrous veins of the fin in a spurt of blood.

The mate comes back with the bucket of barbed J-hooks. Pat pushes sliced bloody dolphin meat onto the hooks. She wipes sweat off her face and looks up. "Perfect bait— the turtles always think it's drifting squid."

Pat goes into the pilothouse and throws the engine switch. The engine growls to life in a loud metallic clang of firing pistons. She steers the boat out on a new course. The mate feeds the baited hooked longline off the stern into the slashed V-wake of the propeller-churned water behind the boat. The longline whirrs away into the distance, sinking from sight beneath the water.

The sun smacks down on Pat at the back of her boat; she is cranking the wood handle of the line-winch, which reels in the longline trailing in the water. The mate works next to her, hoisting the longline onto the deck. All the longline's barbed hooks are stripped of dolphin bait. Pat keeps cranking the handle; the veins on her neck pop out purple. The last of the longline left in the water jerks, goes taut, whirs back out. Pat grips the handle tighter, puts all of her strength into trying to stop the line from stripping farther out behind the boat. The mate grabs the handle with Pat. They strain together, groaning as their muscles burn, holding the longline. The tension reverses toward Pat and the mate; they crank the winch handle harder. The longline in the water comes closer to the boat.

The gray humped shell of a sea turtle crests above the water. The steel barbs of a J-hook are sunk deep into one of its thrashing front flippers. The turtle aggressively flaps its free flipper against the water's surface, struggling to turn its great weight against the hook that holds it to the taut line.

Pat whoops with joy. "A leatherback! Jackpot!"

The mate holds the winch handle steady.

Pat grabs a heavy net. She leans off the side of the boat and casts the net across the water over the splashing turtle. She holds the rope attached to the net as the turtle's bulk thrusts against its sudden entrapment.

The mate jams the winch handle into the locked position. He joins Pat in holding the net rope against the fury of the turtle. They are pulled to the edge of the boat. They lean dangerously off the side of the boat, about to fall into the water, pitting their combined weight against the turtle. A mighty thrust from the turtle knocks Pat and the mate off balance, and they fall to their knees on the slippery deck. They hang on to the rope, pulling back harder, groaning as they haul the turtle up from the water and heft it aboard. The turtle's bulk crashes onto the deck in a booming thump, its massive shell glistening; its prehistoric sharp-beaked face snaps from side to side as it gasps in exertion with humanlike sounds.

Pat gazes at the formidable animal before her. "What a beauty. Must be a hundred years old. Big money in the fin meat. Chinese are convinced eating it will give them King Kong hard-ons to bang their girly friends all night long." She throws her head back, joyfully singing out at the top of her lungs an old pop song, *"All night long, forever!"*

The mate wipes sweat off his tattooed chest. "Yeah, Chinese will pay a fortune."

The turtle powerfully slaps its long leathery flippers against the deck, futilely searching for water to make its escape. The hollow gasping from its beaked mouth becomes desperate; its bulging sea-green eyes gape up at its captors.

Pat picks up an iron mallet and grips its handle. She mounts the netted turtle. Her legs straddle both sides of the humped shell body. She raises the iron mallet, takes aim at the back of the turtle's exposed head, and swings. The mallet penetrates deep into the turtle's skull with a bone-shattering blow.

The mate stares at the turtle's crushed skull. His face cracks into a downward frown. He turns and leans over the railing of the boat, spewing an arc of vomit into the water.

From her perch atop the dead turtle's massive shell, Pat swings the bloody mallet high and shouts with a laugh at the mate, "Man up, you pussy!"

Joan sits on the edge of her bed. The soft curves of her body are outlined through a sheer slip. She tilts her head and listens to approaching footsteps in the hallway. She looks anxiously at the closed bedroom door as it creaks open. A figure comes through the doorway.

Luz steps into the room. "Sorry I'm late, hon." She unbuckles her pistol and sets it on the dresser. She pulls off her shoes and trousers and stands in her loose white shirt and white panties. She begins to unbutton her shirt and notices the concerned expression on Joan's face. She speaks in a soothing voice: "You can stop worrying, I'm home."

"I can't help worrying. I know what's going on."

"What do you mean, you know what's going on?"

"Since Nina became ill, you've changed. You hardly touch me anymore. Nina is my tragedy too."

Luz gets down on her knees before Joan. Her sad eyes stare apologetically. "You're right. I'm sorry. I just can't . . . get beyond . . . this pain."

"There is only one way out of pain. You have to push it aside with new life." Joan takes the bottom of her slip with her fingers. She sensually glides the slip up over the swell of her hips, past the thinness of her waist, and above her arched breasts. She pulls the slip over her head and tosses it aside. The white skin of her face flushes pink as her lips part, offering Luz her mouth for a kiss.

Luz leans toward Joan, then stops. "Forgive me, darling. I can't."

Joan slides an arm around Luz's waist and pulls her close. She covers Luz's face with lip-brushing kisses. Luz's breath sucks in sharply with a gasp. Joan lies back on the bed, her arms outstretched, the fullness of her naked body exposed. Her breasts heave; her rib cage expands and contracts with deep, expectant breathing. She reaches up and gently pulls Luz's head down.

Luz's cheek rests on Joan's smooth thigh. She inhales the sweetness of Joan's skin. She listens to Joan's urgent breathing. She hears the sound of her own breath. She tastes the wet saltiness of her tears as they fall from her eyes. The tears run down Joan's thigh, disappearing into a shadowed crevice.

Ceiling fans swirl in the humid air over the heads of Big Conch and Hard Puppy, who are perched on stools at the Bounty Bar's long counter. Their eyes are riveted on Zoe, dressed in her work uniform of tight white shorts and white halter top. She stands in front of the cash register, adding up the night's receipts.

Hard swings around to Big. The left side of his forehead has a red gash where Luz whacked him with the butt of her gun. His platinum teeth flash as he drunkenly slurs his words into Big's face. "Only be two things in life you need to know. First be, how to get along with people. Second be, how to get around people."

Big slams his beer bottle on the mahogany counter. "Thousand fucking times you told me that. I hear it again, I'm going to bash your—"

Zoe interrupts. "Time to go, Boy Scouts. I'm closing."

Big throws a questioning look across the counter at Zoe. "I'm always thinking, why's a lovely lady like you running a bar?"

Zoe gives a weary smile. "Every time you're here drinking, you ask that. It's always the same answer: I have a university degree in philosophy. Can't do anything with that except teach or tend bar. I had to support Noah through law school, couldn't do that on a teacher's salary. So here I am, still in the bar racket."

Big keeps his questioning going, enjoying the beer buzz-cut of his words. "That Truth Dog of yours is a drinking man, sucks it up like a thirsty baby, but never comes in here. He stays away because he knows Big rules this roost. Your Dog's a chickenshit."

Zoe walks from the register to Big. She stares at his blurry, reddened blue eyes. "Okay, Big, I'll tell you with no philosophizing why Noah is never here. You're an amateur drinker—you drink in public places. Noah is a professional. A professional, he drinks alone. He doesn't need an audience."

Hard nods his head in agreement with Zoe. He digs a

coin out of his pocket. He flips the coin in the air, catches it, and closes his fist on it. He holds out his clenched fist to Zoe. "What side my coin be comin' down on? Be it heads, you go home with me. Be it tails, you go home with Big. You call it, bitch goddess."

Zoe shrugs her shoulders and laughs. "You can keep flipping that coin until it loses its shine. I'm not going home with either of you." She quickly scoops up Hard's and Big's beer bottles. "Time to leave, guys. No more telling each other true lies."

Hard shifts his gaze to the end of the counter, where Hogfish sits alone, his head jerking erratically to music pumping through iPhone earbuds. Hard turns back to Zoe and gives her a mocking wink. "I gets it now. You be savin' yourself for the Hog. That guy can barely make a bologna sandwich with what little pink meat he's got between the legs."

Big belches in Hogfish's direction. "What's left of his brain has been boiled like a lobster in a pot."

Zoe moves down to Hogfish and leans across the counter to him. "Sorry, camper. Two o'clock at night. I want to close up shop. You'll have to leave." Hogfish's glazed eyes roll; he doesn't look at Zoe. She pulls the earbuds out of his ears. "I said you have to go." He snatches the earbuds back from her, jumps off the barstool, and runs for the door.

Hard hoots as the door slams behind Hogfish. "That sucka be a spook! Spookier than his crazy ol' man!"

Big slaps his open palm on the counter and hooks a macho grin at Zoe. "If Hog ever hassles you, give Big the word. I'll snip his balls off and run them up the flagpole."

Zoe walks back along the counter and stops in front of Big. "I don't need you to protect me, not from Hogfish, not from anyone."

Big's grin widens to a belligerent smirk. "I'm serious as a triple heart bypass. Hog gets a weird-on with you, just nod in Big's direction and he's dust."

Zoe pushes away from Big. "Hogfish isn't hassling me. Leave the poor guy alone. It's Hogfish that's being hassled. Hassled by the world. That's what happens to these vets that come back from wars they didn't start. I know. My father got the same treatment when he came back from Vietnam, treated like shit or ignored like a freak. Cut Hogfish some slack or this bitch goddess will scrape those blue eyes out of your head with her pretty fingernails."

Big throws his head back and shouts up at the fan blades cutting the air, "Goddamn, ain't nothing sexier than a sassy woman!" He looks back at Zoe. "You're a spur under my saddle, but I still want to ride you. Ride your gorgeous ass right into the sunset!"

Zoe steps outside beneath a neon BOUNTY BAR sign glowing blue above her in the humid night air. She locks the bar's front door, puts the key in her purse, and zips the purse up. She tucks the purse under her arm and starts walking away. She stops, hearing shuffling from the other side of the deserted street. She looks across the street and stares into the shadows of a tall night-blooming cactus tree. She sees no movement. She glances up at the hanging orange lantern of the moon with halos of light thickening around it, indicating rain is close. She continues walking, heading along empty palm-lined streets snaking between century-old white clapboard houses with wraparound balconies and widows' walks, once inhabited by ship captains and harbor customs men, now tarted up in shiny new tropical colors and surrounded by the electrical drone of motors powering air conditioners and backyard swimming-pool pumps. The houses are constructed cheek by jowl; their tall pitched tin roofs lean into one another as if to block any hurricane winds that might come rushing unannounced through the streets.

Zoe hears the fall of footsteps behind her. She stops beneath the leafy canopy of a woman's-tongue tree. She spins quickly around and looks back to surprise whoever might be following her. She sees no one; she waits. She hears above her the rattle of seeds in the long pods dangling from the woman's-tongue tree. The air brings the scent of a rotting dead rat. She hears footsteps again. She stays still. Her breathing becomes faster, her heart pounds. She smells her own fear exuding with the perspiration from her exposed skin. She jolts at a sudden screeching. She hears a thump from the porch of the house across the street. The entwined bodies of two black cats locked together in lust roll off the porch as they scream in sharp pain.

Zoe turns and walks on at a faster pace, her long legs in her white shorts flashing in the night. Nocturnal skink lizards on the cracked sidewalk skitter away. The sound of footsteps behind her grows louder. She doesn't look back as she hurries to her two-story Bahamian-style house with its smooth plastered exterior of blush-pink walls and framed white windows. She opens the gate of the picket fence in front of her house and races up the flagstone steps. She unlocks the door, steps inside, and slams the door closed.

In the jungle-thick garden behind Zoe's two-story house, insects chirp and frogs croak in the dense foliage. The insects and frogs suddenly fall silent as oncoming footsteps sound. A person's heavy breathing wafts through the air.

A light inside Zoe's house goes on from the second-story bedroom facing the garden. Through the bedroom's open window, golden lamplight illuminates her as she hurriedly undresses. She stands naked for a moment, then quickly slips on a silk robe. A sudden gust of wind bangs the wooden plantation shutters against the sides of her bedroom window. She leans out from the window and grabs the wooden shutters. She is caught framed by light behind her; the wind blows her hair and flutters her silk robe. Her robe falls open, exposing the swing of her breasts. She grabs the open robe and pulls it tightly together. She slams the shutters closed.

In the garden, wind rustles the jungle foliage. The noise of insects and frogs starts again. Thunder rumbles overhead; lightning bolts crack the darkness and expose in the garden the upturned body of a Cuban death's-head palmetto roach. Red fire ants swirl up from the earth around the brown-crusted hoary creature and begin devouring its multitude of legs flailing hopelessly. Rain shoots down from the sky.

Rain slashes onto Pat's boat, anchored at the shrimping-boat dock. Pat, belowdecks, in a narrow berth, tosses and turns in her sleep. The rain above awakens her. Illuminated numbers on a digital clock next to her glow: 4:02.

A clanging bang from the deck above startles her. She jumps out of the berth and pulls on her clothes. She grabs a flashlight and a sharp fish-boning knife. She shines the beam before her as she climbs the spiral galley ladder to the top deck and steps cautiously out into the rain. She aims the beam in the darkness. The beam illuminates a long rope from the mainmast that was ripped loose by the wind and dangles down. At the rope's end is a steel pulley, clanging against the deck.

Pat struggles to secure the rope back to the mast in the wind and rain. She ties the rope down, then shines the beam around the boat again. Nothing seems wrong, she goes below. Rain continues to pound on the empty deck.

On the side of Pat's boat, at the waterline, next to the heavy iron anchor chain, the skull head of a black-and-white-rubber-encased skeleton emerges from the water. The head turns slowly, revealing an iridescent skeleton face with two deep black eye sockets. Hard rain drums on the skeleton's face.

The skeleton's black-rubber-gloved fingers rise from the water and grab the anchor chain. The skeleton pulls out of the water, climbs hand over hand up the length of the anchor chain, and stands upright on the deck of the boat. Slung over the skeleton's shoulder is a speargun. The rain beats on the skeleton as it moves stealthily across the wet deck. It stops before the closed galley door leading belowdecks. The skeleton does not move. It waits. The rain whips harder, thwacking against the skeleton's tight rubber suit. The skeleton's bony-fingered rubber hand reaches out slowly and clutches the latch of the galley door. It slides the door back, steps silently through the opening, and closes the door behind.

Halfway down the inside galley spiral ladder leading belowdecks, the flash of a thrown knife whirs past the descending skeleton. The tip of the knife's blade drives deep into the wood wall behind the skeleton's skull. The skeleton peers from its deep eye sockets into the surrounding darkness. Out of the darkness Pat appears, her breath bursting in a war-cry as she runs, swinging the barbed hook of a gaffing pole before her with a muscular hurl. The skeleton dives into the shadows. Pat's gaffing pole swipes through the air, its flashing steel hooks seeking their target.

On the boat's deck above, the wind howls in the rigging and around the tall mast. The wind picks up velocity; its howl becomes a high-pitched sound like screaming, screaming lost to all ears in the fury of a raging storm.

The morning glare exposes the shrimping-boat dock blocked off by police cars and yellow crime-scene tape; screeching seagulls circle above. On the deck of Pat's boat, a team of latex-gloved investigators work methodically, gathering evidence. Among them are Luz and the Police Chief, scrutinizing a red **X** spray-painted on the deck's plank flooring. The Chief glances at Luz with a look of dismay. "I was hoping Bizango had moved on."

Luz stares at the boat's boom net extended over the water. "No such luck. He's back in business." Tangled inside the net hanging from the boom is Pat's naked, bloody body. A steel spear is pierced between her breasts, through her chest, and out her back. Her ears have been cut off. Her lifeless lips are closed shut by the sharp barbed metal points of J-hooks.

The Chief shakes his head. "Only thing different with Bizango's MO this time is, he closed the mouth with J-hooks, not fishing line. Why J-hooks?"

"Could be simple. Could be that's all he had."

"J-hooks, for Christ's sake. I still don't get it."

A rowboat in the water below the boom glides under the net weighted with Pat's body. A police photographer in the boat aims his camera up and rapid-fires pictures through a zoom lens.

The Chief looks at the seagulls above, diving in downward swoops toward the mutilated body in the net. "Why Pat? She's not involved with Neptune Bay Resort."

"No rhyme or reason. Bizango must be—"

Loud shouting and banging come from belowdecks.

Luz and the Chief run to the open hatch doorway leading below. They pull their guns and climb down the spiral ladder into the galley. They look around; the galley is deserted. They hurry through a low opening into the engine room. Next to a maze of greasy valves, pistons, and pipes stands Moxel, holding a gun to the head of the Haitian boy Rimbaud.

Moxel triumphantly announces, "Found this monkey hiding here."

Rimbaud's fatigued red eyes are terrified, his clothes dirty and ragged; his body is thin from lack of food.

The Chief rushes to Rimbaud. "What did you do to the white woman? How long have you been hiding on her boat?"

Rimbaud is too frightened to answer. He looks with pleading wide eyes at Luz.

Luz steps close to Rimbaud and speaks in a calm voice. "Son, what's your name?"

Rimbaud bites his trembling lip and doesn't answer.

"Son, I promise I won't let them hurt you. Who are you?"

Rimbaud's words blurt out in French to Luz. "Protect me! I saw a Bizango. Don't let Bizango kill me."

The Chief looks at Luz. "What's he saying?"

Moxel shouts. "Yeah, what's the monkey's alibi!"

Luz shakes her head. "I don't know what he's saying. He seems to be speaking French. All I understand is the word 'Bizango.'"

The Chief orders Luz, "Lock him up and get him an interpreter. I want answers."

Moxel unhooks the steel handcuffs dangling from his

belt. He grabs Rimbaud's thin arms and roughly shackles the boy's hands behind his back. He pushes the boy forward with a proud nod at the Chief and Luz. "I'll book him. It was me. I got Bizango. I got the serial killer."

Luz paces back and forth impatiently at the end of a long corridor in the Detention Center. A uniformed and armed guard marches to her with Rimbaud. The boy's head is shaved; his skinny body looks lost in a bright-orange prisoner jumpsuit; his hands are cuffed.

The guard speaks to Luz quickly, with irritation: "Where's the interpreter? He's supposed to be here to get the prisoner's statement."

"Don't worry. He's coming. Take the handcuffs off the boy."

"No way. He's a murder suspect."

Luz sees Noah, dressed in his rumpled seersucker suit, weaving drunkenly up the corridor. He stops in front of her and raises his hand in a salute. "French interpreter, reporting for duty, sir."

Luz stiffens with anger. "Sober up! This kid's being accused of murder! You've got a job to do!"

Noah turns and recognizes the shaven-head prisoner in the orange jumpsuit. He blurts out a laugh. "Rimbaud! He's no murderer. You've got to be kidding. The kid is harmless. What kind of bullshit is this?"

The guard sniffs the rum scent of Noah's breath. "It's no bullshit, buddy. You have thirty minutes to get the prisoner's statement before he's locked up again."

Noah tilts on wobbly legs. "A whole thirty minutes, how generous. With that much time I can get his entire life story and also read him *Moby-Dick*."

The guard takes Rimbaud by the arm and pulls him across the hall. He shoves Rimbaud through an open doorway into a windowless room, then looks back at Noah. "You're wasting time. Now you only have twenty-nine minutes. Get in here."

Noah walks across the hall and steps inside the room. The guard walks out and shuts the door behind him.

Noah and Rimbaud sit across from each other at a bare table. Rimbaud's bony jaw is set; his lips are clamped shut.

Noah takes out a black micro–digital recorder from his coat pocket. He sets the recorder on the table, turns it on, and speaks to Rimbaud in French. "I'm glad you're alive. I'd given up hope. Why did you leave my boat the night of the Shrimp Fleet Blessing?"

Rimbaud's eyes turn down. He stares at the bare wood surface of the table and doesn't answer.

Noah slips out a pint bottle of rum from his other coat pocket. He takes a swallow and sets the bottle next to the micro-recorder. "Rimbaud, help me out. They're holding you for murder. Why did you leave my boat? You were safe there."

Rimbaud keeps staring at the tabletop. With his index finger, he traces out on the table's surface an invisible spiraling circle.

"Listen, kid, I know what you've been through. You escaped the misery of Haiti and drifted on a rickety raft seven hundred miles in shark-infested waters to make it to this promised land. You lost your home, your family, everything, the same old sad story. There's nothing going to change the sad story unless you let me help you. Tell me, why did you leave my boat?"

Rimbaud's head snaps up, his eyes wild with fear, his French words shrill. "To save myself! I jumped from your boat because the sky was exploding with fire!"

"The sky exploding? What do you mean? Ah, the celebration fireworks that were being shot off that night. It never occurred to me you'd never seen fireworks before. No wonder it scared the hell out of you." Noah urges Rimbaud on with another question. "What happened after you left my boat?"

Rimbaud squirms, trying to make himself smaller inside his oversized orange jumpsuit. His words come out slowly. "I hid . . . on different . . . boats."

"So that's why you were on Pat's boat."

"Pat?"

"The woman whose boat you were found on."

A loud knock raps on the closed door. From behind the door, the guard's voice shouts, "Be quick. Hurry up."

Noah looks directly into Rimbaud's eyes. "Did you kill Pat?"

Rimbaud moves forward in his chair. He speaks in a low voice, afraid of being overheard.

Noah leans in, struggling to hear the barely audible words coming from Rimbaud's trembling lips.

"One night, a skeleton rose from the dead. I was hiding, and I saw it with my own eyes. I saw Bizango."

"Bizango? Who is Bizango?"

"A skeleton who rises from the dead. A zombie executioner. He is the great corrector between right and wrong, between good and evil. He is the ultimate judge. Bizango kills evil people."

"You're telling me a zombie skeleton rose from the dead and killed Pat?"

Rimbaud stares fearfully and nods his head in an emphatic yes.

Noah turns off the micro-recorder. He picks up his bottle and takes a long drink. He caps the bottle and slips it back into his pocket. He fixes Rimbaud with a solemn gaze. "I know you're innocent, kid, but if the only defense you have is that you saw a zombie kill Pat, then you'll be convicted for murder."

A cloaked judge stares down from her elevated podium at the defendant's table below, where Noah sits between Rimbaud and a young public defender. Behind the table stands a uniformed bailiff with a holstered .45 strapped to his waist. From the back row of benches, Luz leans forward intently, watching the proceedings in the crowded courtroom.

The judge dips her glasses low on her nose and glowers at Noah. "Because of your past inappropriate antics in a Florida court, you have been disbarred from practicing law in this state. What are you doing in my courtroom?"

The public defender quickly rises and answers in a nervous voice: "Your Honor, may I clarify that Noah Sax is not here as legal representation for the defendant. I am the defendant's counsel. I respectfully would like to make a motion to the court that—"

The judge cuts the young defender off. "These proceedings will not continue with Mr. Sax present." She nods to the bailiff. "Escort Mr. Sax from my courtroom."

The armed bailiff steps to Noah and pulls him up by the arm from his chair. Noah shakes free from the bailiff and faces the judge. "I'm not here as an attorney. I'm here as the defendant's interpreter. The defendant has a right to an interpreter of his—"

The judge jabs her finger at Noah. "It's at the court's discretion to appoint the interpreter. I certainly did not appoint you."

"But under Florida law the defendant has a right to an interpreter of his own choosing. It specifically sets forth in State Statute Number—"

"Mr. Sax, don't push your luck. If you're out of order here today, I'll jail you for contempt."

"Count on me, Your Honor, I'll be a model citizen."

"No wisecracks. I won't tolerate it. If it were possible to disbar you twice, I would."

Noah sits back down between Rimbaud and the defense attorney.

The judge bangs her gavel. "This hearing is postponed until the autopsy of the deceased victim, Pat Judy Benson, is complete. The defendant, Rimbaud Mesrine, is to be held without bail."

Noah jumps up. "That's not fair. If it please the court, I would like to—"

"No, it does not please this court. Nothing you do will ever please this court. Be seated."

Noah stays on his feet. "I just wanted to say that I have information from the defendant regarding—"

The judge glares. "No more warnings, Mr. Sax. I'm locking you up right now if you don't shut up."

The defense attorney rises quickly. "Your Honor, if it please the court, may I—"

"Counsel, I already told Mr. Sax, this court is not pleased!"

The judge bangs her gavel. "Court adjourned!"

Beneath the sway of palm trees the cemetery is a crowded maze of granite gravestones and cement-plastered tombs bleached by the sun to an otherworldly bone-white. Family plots are decorated with reposing stone lambs, winged angels in alabaster, and limestone Christian crosses. Tall white-feathered ibises stalk ghostlike on spindly legs across the sparse grassy turf. The birds' long curved bills are held ready as they stare down to peck a scuttling brown roach or squirming grub. On top of a twenty-foot marble obelisk, a red-shouldered hawk is perched, alert for rodent prey among the bouquets of faded plastic flowers scattered in the weeds of unkempt graves. The hawk swivels its head and stares down from its lofty perch at Luz below, as she follows a meandering pathway through the city of the dead. Luz pushes Nina in her wheelchair; Chicken trots alongside. Luz stops and looks up at the hawk on the point of the obelisk. The hawk stares back with amber eyes and screeches a high-pitched whistle.

Nina's thin fingers nervously fidget with the stems of the fresh bouquet of white lilies held in her lap. She gazes at the hawk and winces. "It won't hurt us, will it, Mom?"

"Not unless you're a mouse, honey. Nothing to worry about."

"Well, with no hair on my head, my ears look really, really big. Maybe the hawk will think I'm Minnie Mouse."

Luz smiles at Nina's lightheartedness. The hawk whistles shrilly again. It spreads its wings and wheels off the granite point, soaring from sight into the blur of sun-bleached sky.

Luz continues pushing Nina down a path between rows of old and neglected graves with tilted and crumbling headstones. She stops Nina's wheelchair at a well-kept site beneath the lacy green spread of a poinciana tree in full bloom with sashes of red flowers. The names carved into the surrounding headstones all read ZAMORA. Luz kneels and makes the sign of the cross. Her eyes mist over, and her lips move reverentially in silent prayer. Nina hands Luz the bouquet of lilies. Luz places one lily before each of the Zamora headstones and turns to Nina. "Our family has been on this island for five generations. We'll be the last Zamoras buried here. After us the cemetery will be full up—no more plots left, even for the grandchildren of Cuban heroes."

"I know, Mom. You tell me that each time we come here. But I don't want to think about where I'll be buried, it's creepy."

"Tradition is important. Tradition makes us all part of one another, part of something bigger. I don't want you to forget your heritage. There were slaves in Cuba. Zamoras fought against Spain to free Cuba in the 1868 rebellion. That's the problem today."

"What do you mean, that's the problem today?"

"No one is willing to sacrifice. No one is—"

Luz notices Chicken sniffing aggressively, his nose pointed at a gnarly blob of a toad with bulging eyes and a milky substance foaming from its fat, warty lips. The toad squats in the grass next to a Zamora grave. Chicken stiffens, prepared to attack. Luz grabs the dog by the collar and pulls him back. "That's a Bufo toad. He's poisonous. One bite of him and you're dead."

Chicken barks, but not at the toad. He sees a dark figure outlined by the sun's glare approaching through the gravestones. Chicken growls as the figure comes closer. It is Moxel. He stops in front of Luz, panting from the heat, the armpits of his blue uniform dampened by sweat rings. His words rush out hoarse from his dry throat. "I was just at your house. Joan told me you'd be here. The Chief wants you in his office." Moxel glances down at Nina. "How you doing, little girl? Your mom should know better than to bring someone in your condition out in this hundred-degree heat. This sun will turn your skin blacker than charcoal."

The toad next to a grave in the grass springs up and takes two lunging hops toward Moxel. He squints in the glaring sunlight at the toad. "What's that ugly-ass frog?"

Luz keeps her hand tight on Chicken's collar as the dog strains to get at the toad. "Poisonous. Don't touch it."

"Poisonous, no shit." Moxel unsnaps his side holster, yanks out his revolver, and shoots, blasting the toad. Toad fragments spew into the air and splatter across the carved name ZAMORA on a headstone. Nina screams and cringes in her wheelchair. Moxel shoves his gun back into its holster and grins. "I hope I didn't blow away an endangered species."

Luz spins Nina's wheelchair around so Nina can't see her whip her Magnum from its holster. She jams the pistol's barrel into the side of Moxel's head. "You are an endangered species."

Inside the Police Chief's office, the Chief and Moxel stop their animated conversation as Luz enters. Moxel's face reddens as he blurts at Luz: "You pulled a gun on me for shooting a frog! What the fuck is that? I'm the one who saved your ass in the bat tower. If I hadn't climbed up that ladder and risked my life to help you, you would have fallen to your death." Moxel swings around to the Chief. "What kind of force is this if she's allowed to pull a gun on another officer? You should fire her for unfit conduct. You should—"

The Chief cuts Moxel off. "Calm down. I don't have time for fraternal squabbles." He turns to Luz and hands her a thick folder of papers. "This forensic report just came in. The Haitian kid's fingerprints were found all over Pat's boat."

Luz takes the thick folder. "I'll read it. What about Pat's body? Were Rimbaud's fingerprints found on her body?"

"No, nothing. Maybe the kid was wearing gloves."

"Rimbaud told the interpreter he saw Bizango on the boat. Did the lab find any trace of that?"

"Zip, no fingerprints, no hair, no footprints, no nothing. If Bizango was on that boat, he doesn't just wear gloves, he must be dressed in a glove. Only prints found were from the Haitian and Pat's boat mate. You got something on the mate?"

"Found him up the Keys at the Pink Grouper strip club in Marathon. Checked out his alibi. Says he was at the club the night of the murder."

"Witnesses to that?"

"All six of the pole dancers who performed that night. One of them says he shoved a hundred-dollar bill beneath her panties, up her butt hole."

"Good to know some guys are still gentlemen."

Luz looks curiously at the report folder. "Anything in here about the hooks puncturing Pat's lips?"

"Mustad Super Marlin J-hooks. No prints on them, but we hit a different jackpot." The Chief picks up a black micro–digital recorder from his desk. "A recorder like this was found inside Pat's mouth."

Luz eyes the recorder. "Same kind found in Bill Warren's mouth at the bat tower. There's a Bizango recording on it?"

"Yeah, but saying something different."

"Is it in English, like the Bill Warren recording?"

"Of course, why?"

"Because Rimbaud only speaks French. I know this for a fact. He can't be Bizango if this recording is in English."

Moxel snorts derisively. "Did you ever think that somebody else recorded it for him? There could be a team of Bizangos operating in Key West."

Luz moves closer to the Chief. "Maybe we should go public with the recordings. Can't let this grow cold. We need anything we can get."

"No, Moxel might be correct. If there are two Bizangos, I don't want to give the other one the advantage of knowing we are stumped. That's what he wants—he wants these recordings to be broadcast. Besides, the public is already frightened enough about the murders, they're all over the news."

"But somebody in the public might have important information, a lead."

"There's another reason to keep a lid on these killings. Eighty thousand big spenders are headed here for the Halloween Fantasy Parade. I won't be held responsible for destroying the island's biggest payday of the year."

"You could be right. Play the recording."

The Chief turns around to Moxel. "I want only Luz to hear this recording, it's highly sensitive. Close the door on your way out."

Moxel doesn't budge. "Only Luz? Why her? I'm on this investigation too. I'm the one who busted the Haitian."

Luz looks at Moxel and nods toward the door. "You heard, go."

Moxel stares defiantly at Luz. "I want to hear the recording. Maybe that Haitian monkey is faking it and he really does speak English. Did you ever think of that, Mrs. Sherlock Holmes?"

The Chief shouts angrily at Moxel. "You're out of line! Leave!"

Moxel shuffles past Luz, knocking hard against her shoulder. He opens the door, and the sound of its slamming behind him fills the room.

The Chief shrugs and looks apologetically at Luz. "He's loyal but stupid."

"You mean he's stupid but loyal."

"Anyway, he's gone."

The Chief cocks his thumb over the micro-recorder's play button. "Now you'll understand why I don't want this going public. It's much worse than the recording found in Warren's mouth." He presses his thumb down forcefully on the recorder's play button.

Noah's trawler floats in the middle of the ocean, under a sky of high, drifting clouds. He sits in the pilothouse, in front of his jerry-rigged radio broadcast console, listening intensely to an irate caller.

"America is swamped by boat people, illegal refugees, undocumented workers, political-asylum seekers. These people are on the shit end of life's stick. If we reach out to them, we'll be covered in their shit."

Noah answers in a steady voice: "I don't agree with you. I recently saw a refugee raft from Haiti come in. People on that raft were not covered in shit, they were scorched to death by the sun in their desperate attempt to escape famine, disease, and fear." He stops talking and picks up the rum bottle sitting on the console table. He takes a swig and continues. "The rickety raft I saw would have had a hard time making it across a hotel pool in Miami, let alone across seven hundred miles of open ocean between here and Haiti. But you know what, it's better to swim with sharks in the sea than be eaten by menacing, pathological, corrupt politicians on land. Next caller. You're on pirate radio."

"Hey, hot damn, I'm on."

"The soap box is yours, pilgrim. Go."

"Stop squawking about dead Haitian illegals when there's three Americans murdered recently right here in Key West. Talk about something real. Nobody's safe in Key West."

"I don't talk about those murders because they're plastered all over the newspapers and TV twenty-four/seven. What's interesting, though, is that the first two murders were Neptune Bay partners but the third victim was a boat captain. No coherent pattern. You're right, nobody's safe, but when were we ever really safe? Next caller."

A deep male voice rumbles. "*Hola,* Truth Dog, this is the Nam vet. Today's the day I'm goin' to tell you how it's all goin' to end. The Permian Extinction Event in the Gulf!"

The pilothouse of Noah's trawler suddenly sways hard side to side. The cell phones on his console table slide off and hit the floor. He grips the table's edge and holds on as the boat rocks. Outside the pilothouse window, a cruise ship steams by; its turbo diesel engines roar, creating a huge wake. The ship's twenty-story-high bulk blocks the sun, pitching Noah's pilothouse into darkness. He keeps his hands gripped on the edge of the console.

Sunlight floods back into the pilothouse as the trawler stops rocking. Noah regains his balance. He looks outside and sees the name of the departing cruise ship painted on its white stern, *Titan Reef.*

He rearranges his three fallen cell phones back on the console table and turns them on. The red lights of the phones flash with incoming calls. He reconnects the microphone wire. He slows his heavy breathing to even out his anxiety and speaks calmly into the microphone. "Listeners, you just lost me there. I was almost the hit-and-run victim of a cruise ship, the *Titan Reef*, headed for Key West. I was like a Chihuahua going up against King Kong. Give me a minute while I adjust my speaker volume controls." He looks around for his rum bottle and sees it on the floor. He picks up the bottle, uncaps it, and takes a long slug. He leans back into the microphone. "The cruise ships always sail too close to the coral reefs. You've heard me talk about the *Titan Reef* before. Last year it plowed right through a Caribbean atoll. What took nature millions of years to create was destroyed in one moment. There's no reason for these ships to wreak environmental catastrophe. The captains know their nautical coordinates. They're just taking shortcuts to save fuel. The *Titan Reef* captain who buzz-sawed his ship's massive propellers through that atoll was not fired. His company paid off some government officials. That captain is a criminal who committed willful manslaughter against nature. He should be hauled before a world tribunal, should be made to walk the plank at the sharp end of a sword. Accountability, pilgrims, brings the bastards to justice."

All the red phone lights flash with calls. Noah punches through one of the lines. A woman's voice singsongs with exasperation. "Those monster ships shouldn't be sailing these waters. They weigh more than a hundred thousand tons; they've got tennis courts, shopping malls, bowling alleys, movie megaplexes. People aren't satisfied building that stuff on land, they've got to float it out on the ocean too."

"Right. Next caller. Show me the rage."

From the big wooden speakers explodes an eerie, electronically altered voice.

"Truth Dog, you say you broadcast the truth!"

Noah is startled by the weird voice but snaps back: "I say I let people speak their own truth. Who is this? What's with the audio masquerade? Use your own voice if you're so interested in truth."

"I'm challenging you. You keep a photograph of a woman in the drawer beneath your radio console."

"How did you know that?"

"Open the drawer."

Noah pulls open the wooden drawer beneath the console. In the drawer is a framed photograph of Zoe. He takes out the photograph. "So you know where I keep a photograph of my wife. When were you on my boat?"

"Turn the photograph over."

Noah flips the framed photograph over; duct-taped to the back is a CD labeled LAST KEY DEER MANIFESTO. "What the hell? Who is this?"

"If you are not afraid of the truth, play the CD."

Noah rips the CD from the back of the photo frame. "Is this about the endangered Key deer? I'm interested in that."

"Play it."

Noah flicks the disc back and forth between his fingers. The round surface glints with reflected blue and orange light. He leans into the microphone. "Listeners, for you who don't know, the endangered Key deer live only in the Florida Keys. They are small, stand only thirty inches at their shoulders. The Overseas Highway down from Miami runs right through one of their last refuges in Big Pine Key. A sign in Big Pine updates how many Key deer have been slaughtered by speeding cars on the highway each year. The count on that sign for this year is twenty-nine. That means there are fewer than three hundred surviving deer left. Countdown to Armageddon for those little Bambis. At the rate they're being killed, they'll be gone from this earth in a matter of years."

The electronically altered voice jumps with a shout.

"Play the CD!"

Noah looks again at the shards of colored light sparking off the CD held between his fingers. "I'm asking one last time, does this CD have Key-deer information? Otherwise, I'm not interested. I won't be tricked."

"It has the information you want."

Noah pushes the disc into the CD player on the console and punches the volume up. He grabs his bottle of rum, takes a swallow, leans back in his chair, and listens.

An earsplitting crackling static blasts from the big speakers, filling the pilothouse. Cutting through the static is an altered recorded voice reverberating with a metallic echo as if spiraling up from the depths of a steel underground chamber.

"Hear my words, dance my tune.
I am the assassin of lies.
I am the bee in your ear
the scorpion in your bed
the rat clawing in your belly
the knife at your throat
the ax in your back

the sword through your soul
the arrow piercing your heart.
You carry the seeds of your own destruction.
When the atomic dust falls
on your pathetic parade of progress
only I will know the escape route.
I won't let you rocket away from your plunder,
implant a new universe with decay.
You are a virus, I am the eradicating vaccine.
I put on my suit of skeletal lights,
dance into the night to exterminate you.
Are you trembling, crying with fear?
The Key deer you slaughter
on the highway do not cry.
The Key deer heroically struggle
to survive at their final mile zero.
Zero-bop, bop till you drop.
I am the great corrector. I am the ultimate judge.
I am Bizango."

Bizango's raging voice stops. A loud crackling static hisses from the big speakers.

Noah picks up his microphone and shouts into it: "Hey, you, caller, Bizango or whoever you are! You still out there?" Noah looks at the cell phone that the call came in on. The red light is off, the phone is dead. All the phones are dead. "Bizango, call me! I'm ready to rage right back at you!"

Noah watches the phones for an incoming call. No red lights. He continues to wait. No lights. He puts the microphone to his lips. "Bizango, you scared the shit out of everyone; people are afraid to call." He grabs his rum bottle. The bottle is empty. He tosses it aside. "So, my loyal pilgrims, we've had a fun day on trusty old *Noah's Lark.* First there was my near hit-and-run with a *Titanic,* then a weirded-out dude says he's a dancing skeleton coming to slit our throats. I'm sort of out of words. Not that Truth Dog doesn't have any bark and bite left in him—far from it—but sometimes only music can express what we feel. As I head back into Key West, I'll leave you with this music from *Carmina Burana,* a cantata based on the fevered poetry of cloistered thirteenth-century monks. For those of you who don't understand Latin, I'll give you the translation as it plays."

Noah punches out the Bizango CD from the player and pushes in a new disc. "Listen to this, Bizango. Two can play your bloody game. Your kind of evil has been hanging around the school yard of history for a long time."

From the big wood speakers blasts the surge of a majestic soul-wrenching orchestral rhythm accompanied by the aggressive, monumental chant of a male choir. Noah chants his translation over the choir.

> *"Fate,*
> *monstrous and empty*
> *you whirling wheel!*
> *Your malevolent*
> *well-being is vain*
> *and always fades*
> *to nothing!*
> *Shadowed and veiled*
> *you plague me too!*
> *Now through the game*

*I expose my bare back
to
your
villainy!"*

Noah looks through the window of his pilothouse as he motors his trawler toward the distant island outline of Key West. He hears whirring from above. He looks up through the window. A helicopter darts from the sky and swoops in a broad circle over the trawler. On the side door of the helicopter is painted a blue-and-gold insignia: KEY WEST POLICE DEPARTMENT. Inside the copter, the pilot steers the craft, with Luz seated next to him.

Noah cuts his engine and runs from the pilothouse onto the deck. From the copter, Luz's voice booms from a bullhorn: "You're under arrest! Follow me into the harbor!"

Noah waves up to Luz, signaling that he does not understand what is going on. The copter swoops lower, the downward wind of its blades blowing hard against Noah, threatening to sweep him overboard. He sees Luz behind the copter's bulbous window with a rifle gripped in her hands. He struggles against the wind, making his way back into the pilothouse. He grabs the helm and steers toward the island.

The helicopter follows the trawler into the harbor and hovers directly above as Noah pulls up to the dock. He jumps down from the trawler onto the dock and is surrounded by a wall of policemen with rifles pointed at him. The Police Chief pushes his way through the riflemen. He shouts at Noah above the clatter from the helicopter blades. "You think you've been damn clever! I finally got you!" He grabs Noah's hands and handcuffs him.

Noah stares at the Chief in disbelief. "What the hell is going on? You got me for what?"

"This morning you played a Bizango recording that in fact you made. That recording is identical to the one you left in Pat's mouth after you murdered her. No one except the police and the killer knew about that recording. Your pirate-radio charade is over!"

Noah tries to break the grip of the handcuffs binding him. The sharp edges of the cuffs cut into his wrists, drawing blood. "I'm not Bizango!"

The Chief turns to his riflemen. "Read Mr. Truth Dog his Mirandas and lock him up!"

Moonlight shines down over the island's clapboard houses. The modest homes are dwarfed by the immensity of the docked cruise ship, *Titan Reef.* Inside the ship, the sprawling main cocktail lounge is decorated to resemble a big-game African safari camp, its walls crowded with mounted trophy heads of elephants, lions, gazelles, hippos, and rhinos. The amber glass eyes of the dead animals stare down at the carefree passengers sipping exotic cocktails adorned with pink parasol stir-sticks.

The chattering of the passengers stops as the ship's captain struts in dressed in a crisp white mock admiral's uniform with gold-braided epaulettes on the shoulders. He glad-hands the passengers as he works the room with a commanding air. He stops in the center of the room next to an oversized African drum of stretched zebra skin. He bangs on the drum with a carved ebony drumstick. The drum's reverberating bass focuses everyone's attention on him. "I must interrupt your after-dinner soirée. Something important is on the television news I want you to see. I know you've heard reports about some unfortunate murders in Key West, making you have doubts about enjoying a carefree time. This will put your minds at ease while we are berthed here." He holds up a TV remote control and clicks on a wide-screen television spanning the length of a wall between two stuffed leopard heads.

On the TV screen, the Police Chief stands at a podium addressing a crowd of jostling reporters, photographers, and cameramen. His voice is flat and factual. "A suspected serial killer was taken into custody today. I am not at liberty to discuss details. Be assured, the streets of Key West are safe. The annual Fantasy Parade will go forward next week as planned. Those coming here for the world's greatest Halloween party have nothing to fear."

The captain cuts the sound of the Chief's voice with the remote and steps in front of the television screen. "Everyone, you just heard it. Key West is safe. Let's celebrate our good fortune!" The jubilant passengers cheer and raise their cocktail glasses. The captain puffs up to a heroic stance and salutes the crowd. A loud recording of the optimistic tropical song "Don't Worry, Be Happy" fills the air with its upbeat lyrics.

A female passenger in a sexy cocktail dress sways seductively to the captain. She slips her arm intimately around his waist. The woman's laughing husband rapidly fires off the flash of his cell phone in a barrage of photographs of the new couple. The captain dances away with the man's wife.

The captain enters his luxurious suite. He tosses his mock admiral's cap onto a velvet chair and kicks off his shoes. He pulls off his watch and checks its time, 3:30 a.m. He pours himself a Scotch and soda at the elaborate mahogany bar backed by a full-length mirror. As he stirs his drink, he sees reflected in the bar's mirror something approaching from behind. He swings around.

The figure of a black-and-white-rubber-suited skeleton stands before the captain. Clutched in the skeleton's rubber-gloved hands is a speargun, its taut spear in firing position.

The captain holds out his glass of Scotch and soda to the skeleton. "Have a drink, you deserve one—sure as hell fooled me in that disguise. Great costume, but Halloween isn't until next week."

The skeleton remains silent and doesn't move.

The captain sips on his drink. "Let me see your face behind that mask. Must be you, my very special Mike. You're the only one who has a key to my suite."

The skeleton raises the speargun. Its black rubber finger moves to the aluminum trigger. The steel spear fires with a springing whoosh, rams through the captain's chest, into his heart, out his back, and shatters the glass mirror behind in a spray of blood.

The captain falls to the floor, his mouth agape, gasping for air, the spasms of his feet kicking soundlessly into the thick carpeting.

The skeleton reaches down and pushes a black micro-recorder between the captain's lips.

In the gray mist of predawn light, Hard Puppy walks along a fishing pier jutting into Key West Harbor. He pulls behind him on a rope a heavy bloodied burlap sack. He stops at the end of the pier and looks around to check if he is being watched. He waits a few minutes, then unties the sack and exposes the dead body of a black pit bull. The dog's short-haired body is crisscrossed with deep bloody lacerations. Tied to the dog's back legs is a small iron anchor. Hard dumps the dog and anchor out of the sack. The anchor clanks loudly on the concrete pier's surface. He glances around to see if anyone heard. He looks back at the dead pit bull and studies it. He shakes his head and angrily kicks the dog with the pointed tip of his alligator shoe.

The pit bull tumbles off the end of the pier and splashes into the water, sinking under the surface. Its barrel-shaped body bobs back up. Hard's lips pull back in a sneer. "Sink, you bastard. You lost me fifty grand in two fights. Sink, goddamn you."

Around the pit bull's floating body, bubbles appear in the water. The dog slowly sinks again. The iron anchor drags the animal's dead weight down into the depths.

Hard hears screaming. He whips around to see if someone has seen him sink the dog. He spots people running toward a distant pier, where a colossal cruise ship is docked. He kicks the bloody burlap sack into the water, then walks quickly to the distant pier. He joins a crowd at the pier's end. The people stare up the steep steel stern of the ship. The rising sun's light shines on the ship's name, *Titan Reef*. Over the name is slashed in red paint a giant **X**. Swinging in front of the **X** is the captain, his body hung from a rope tight around his neck, his white admiral's uniform soaked through with blood.

Hard looks around at the terrified faces staring up. He breaks into a broad smile. His platinum teeth sparkle in the sun. He saunters away from the dock, snapping his fingers in time to a musical tune that he croons in the voice of an old time Dixie minstrel:

"Goin' to run all de night.
Goin' to run all de day.
Bet me money on a bobtailed nag.
Somebody be bettin' de gray.

Can't touch bottom with a ten-foot pole.
Oh! De doo-da day!"

Deep within the corridors of the massive Detention Center, in a dim isolation cell, Noah sits alone on a cot. He stares at the floor, lines of worry cut across his face. He is startled by the sudden scraping-metal sound of the thick steel cell door behind him swinging open. A shaft of light from outside probes the cell.

Luz appears in the doorway. "You've been freed on bail. There was a Bizango killing last night while you were locked in here."

Noah looks up, bleary-eyed. "So they know I can't be Bizango?"

"They are investigating if you might be his accomplice. The crime lab is getting results from the sweep of your boat and house in their search for anything incriminating. You're still considered a suspect."

"What about Rimbaud? They must be freeing him too?"

"No. Since he was apprehended at the scene of Pat's murder, he's still being held. A trial date has been set."

Noah focuses his eyes hard on Luz. "You had a rifle aimed at me from that helicopter. Were you really going to shoot me?"

"Luckily, I didn't have to decide."

"You believe I'm mixed up in these murders?"

"As someone who knows you, definitely not. As a cop, I have to keep all options open."

"I'm going to find Bizango myself. He used me to get his message out."

"We're dealing with a lethal killer. You're already too involved. Back off or you might end up his next victim." Luz reaches down and pulls Noah up from the cot. "Right now I need you to clean up, shave, and get yourself a new suit for Nina's Quince party. My little girl is turning fifteen tomorrow. You must be there."

"Wouldn't miss it. But just one other thing."

"Yeah?"

"Who made my bail?"

"You don't need to know. It's not important."

Noah grips Luz's shoulder. "It's important to me."

"I promised I wouldn't tell you."

"It's not like I won't find out anyway."

"Okay, Joan. Your sister paid half the bail."

"And?"

"What?"

"The other half. Who paid?"

"Zoe."

Noah steps out from the Detention Center through the front doors. He blinks in the intense sunlight after having been locked up in a windowless cell. On the expanse of asphalt parking lot TV vans with satellite antennas atop their roofs are parked. Reporters and cameramen rush to gather around the Police Chief, recording his words.

"There is no reason for panic. We assure this community that all law-enforcement resources are being used to apprehend the perpetrator of these heinous crimes."

A reporter shouts: "You say no reason to panic, but there have been a string of bizarre killings."

"We had two suspects. One was let go for lack of hard evidence to hold him. We are still holding the other one."

Another reporter yells angrily: "Those two suspects were locked up when the last murder occurred. That means there must be another killer out there. Maybe there's even a team calling themselves Bizango."

"Well, there's at least one Bizango. Next question."

"Is it true the cruise ship's security cameras caught images of the captain's killer?"

"It's true. We have video of whom we believe to be the perpetrator. We also have other important information regarding this investigation that we'll be releasing soon."

"The Fantasy Parade? You going to cancel it now?"

"No. It would take a catastrophic category-five hurricane bearing down on this island before I would cancel the Fantasy Parade. Trust me, every precaution is being taken to keep people on this island safe. I have coordinated with the County Sheriff to put his one hundred fifty deputies on our streets to join with sixty Key West police. Florida Highway Patrol is bringing a canine unit, SWAT team, and one hundred officers. This is an unprecedented show of force."

From behind the circle of reporters surrounding the Chief, Zoe makes her way toward the Detention Center.

She walks up the front steps to where Noah is standing, and stops.

Noah leans forward to give Zoe a kiss on the cheek, rushing her with his words. "Thanks for coming. I didn't expect you to be here when they released me."

Zoe pulls back from Noah's attempted kiss. She lowers the sunglasses covering her eyes and stares over the top rims. "I didn't come here for you. There are still some bail-bond documents I must sign, formalizing the financials of your release."

"I'll pay the money back. Don't worry, I won't jump bail and leave town."

"That's the least I expect from you. But you should know, it's me who's leaving Key West."

Noah hides his surprise and keeps his words steady. "You're leaving? When? You can't go before Nina's Quince. She'll be crushed. She still considers you her aunt."

"I'll be here for Nina. Then, right after the Fantasy Parade, I'm out. Our divorce will be finalized then."

"We're still married. You know, it's not over until it's over."

Zoe gives Noah a radiant smile. "No, it's over."

Luz sits alone on her living-room sofa. The bamboo window shades are drawn against the intense outside tropical light. In the darkened room, her solemn gaze is fixed on a family home movie playing on a television screen. The images flickering across the screen show Luz's living room ten years before, decorated with balloons and ribbons for Nina's birthday party. On the screen, little Nina is a healthy five-year-old wearing a festive paper-cone hat. She leans over a birthday cake with five candles. The red letters on the white-frosted cake spell out HAPPY BIRTHDAY NINA! Nina shuts her eyes tight to make a wish. She blows out the five candles on the cake with a burst of air. She looks up with triumph. Surrounding Nina are Noah, Zoe, Joan, and Carmen, all ten years younger, wearing colorful paper party hats and singing loudly, "Happy birthday to you, dear Nina! Happy birthday to you!" Joan stops singing and speaks at the camera: "Honey, give me the camera. I want to film Nina with her proud mama." The movie image goes out of focus, then refocuses with the image of Luz lifting Nina onto her shoulders. Mother and daughter joyously wave to the camera.

As Luz watches the television screen's flickering images of her and Nina, the muscles of her jaw twitch. She holds back her emotion as Joan comes in and sits close to her. Luz takes Joan's hand. They watch the screen as the five-year-old Nina excitedly opens birthday presents.

Joan's throat tightens. She gets her words out without crying: "Seems like only yesterday. She was so healthy, so full of life."

Luz holds Joan's hand tighter. "Our daughter made it to today's birthday. Every doctor said she wouldn't."

"Why did God do this to her?"

Luz puts her arm around Joan's shoulders. She tries to hide the hurt in her voice. "We can't blame God for Nina's condition."

"I hope we're doing the right thing, having this Quince party."

"We had a fancy hotel Quince for Carmen when she turned fifteen. Even if this one is in our backyard, it will mean the world to Nina."

Joan brushes a tear from her eye. "You're right. It's a miracle she's with us. We do have God to thank for that."

"I count every day of her fifteen years as a blessing. I'll go see how she's holding up. The guests are coming in two hours."

Joan gently touches Luz's cheek. "Are you sure you are okay? Should I go with you?"

"No. I can do it. She's waiting."

Luz leaves Joan and walks down the hallway to Nina's bedroom. The door is open. Inside, a frail Nina sits in her wheelchair, wearing a white Quince-party dress. On her head is a wig of cascading brown ringlets. At her feet is Chicken, curled up and snoring peacefully.

Luz steps into the bedroom. She slips a gift-wrapped box out from her guayabera shirt pocket. She holds the box behind her back as she kneels in front of Nina's wheelchair.

Nina's voice is weak, but her face is animated. "Mom, what's that behind your back?"

"Something for the most special fifteen-year-old girl in the world."

Nina's thin lips turn up in an ironic smile. "I'm special, like the poster child for cancer."

"I didn't mean it that way, darling."

"I know, Mom, I was just kidding. You always say, laughter is our secret weapon."

"You and I, we have a lot of secret weapons."

"So—what's in the box? I bet it's a wedding ring. I bet you're going to show me the wedding ring you're finally giving Joan after twelve years."

"Well, that's an interesting idea."

"You know, you guys should just do it, tie the knot, go on an old-fashioned honeymoon to Niagara Falls."

"You've got my wedding all figured out."

"Carmen and I have it planned."

"It's something to look forward to, but what's in the box is just for you." Luz brings the box from behind her back and offers it to Nina.

"I'm sorry, Mom. I can't open it. My fingers aren't working so well today. You help me with it."

Luz peels off the gift wrapping, exposing a silk jewelry box. She snaps the box open; inside is a gleaming pearl necklace. "Happy fifteenth birthday, darling!"

Nina tries to reach for the pearl necklace, but her arms are too weak.

Luz slips the necklace around Nina's neck and fastens it. The pearls glow in a soft pink halo against Nina's white dress.

Nina beams with pride. "I'm the luckiest girl to have you as my mom."

"It's me who's the lucky one."

"Thank you for such a beautiful gift, and for giving me a party today."

"Nothing could stop me from celebrating this day with you."

Nina's eyelids become heavy, almost closing; the light in her eyes dims. "Mom, can I lie down before the party? I'm so tired. Will you stay with me?"

"Of course—there's time before the guests arrive."

"Are Uncle Noah and Auntie Zoe coming?"

"They wouldn't miss it."

Luz lifts Nina up into her arms from the wheelchair. She lays her on the bed.

Nina's dimming eyes look up. "My wig, Mom. Take my wig off, so it doesn't get crushed before the party."

Luz removes the wig, exposing Nina's bald head. She places the wig carefully on the nightstand and sits on the bed. She caresses Nina's bald head, her fingers stroking back and forth across the smooth skin.

Nina's eyelids flutter. She struggles to keep her eyes open and focused on Luz. "Sing to me, Mom. Sing me your song."

Luz sings in a haunting voice, her words drawn up from a deep well of emotion with melodious melancholy.

"The first time ever I saw your face,
I thought the sun rose in your eyes
And the moon and stars were the gifts you gave
To the dark and the empty skies, my love.
The first time ever I kissed your cheek,
I felt the earth move in my hand
Like the trembling heart of . . ."

Nina's breathing becomes slow and shallow. She sleeps.

Luz and Joan greet the guests in their garden. They give welcoming hugs to the men dressed in colorful slacks and guayabera shirts and kiss the women wearing flowery tropical dresses. Beneath a banyan tree, a banquet table is set with a Cuban feast, a steaming roast pig at its center. Nearby, guests dance on a wooden platform to a snappy Cuban rhythm played by three musicians. Noah stands off to the side of the crowd, tossing a tennis ball to Chicken in a game of fetch.

Nina, wearing her curly brown wig and white Quince-party dress, is wheeled through the merriment in her chair by Carmen. Carmen pushes Nina between guests and stops in front of Noah. He notices the pearl necklace gleaming around Nina's neck. "Who gave you those beautiful pearls?"

Nina blushes with pride. "My mom."

"I'm glad your mom didn't give you one of these, or I'd be out of luck." Noah holds up a delicate watch with a pink patent-leather band. He straps the shiny watchband to Nina's thin wrist and kisses her forehead.

Nina looks with wonder at the watch. "Oh, Uncle, thank you."

"Happy fifteen! You've arrived!"

Carmen looks across the lawn at Zoe, standing in front of a flowering hibiscus bush near the musicians. Carmen turns back to Noah. "Auntie Zoe is over there. How come you aren't dancing with her?"

Noah gazes at Zoe; she is wearing a strapless sundress, her tanned shoulders are bare, her blond hair is swept back. Zoe sways her hips gently to the rhythm of the trio.

Noah nods wistfully. "I don't think Auntie Zoe wants to dance with me."

Carmen rolls her eyes. "Boys can be so clueless."

Nina summons up her strongest voice. "Did you ask her if she wants to dance?"

"No, I didn't."

Nina motions Carmen to lean close to her. She whispers in Carmen's ear. They both giggle. Carmen grabs the back of Nina's wheelchair and pushes Nina away from Noah, across the lawn; she stops in front of Zoe.

Nina blurts out in a flush of excitement to Zoe, "Uncle Noah wants to dance with you!"

Zoe looks across the lawn at Noah throwing the tennis ball for Chicken to chase. "Does he really want to dance? How sweet of you to come and tell me." She reaches into the hibiscus bush behind her and picks two large white flowers. She hands one to Carmen and fixes the other behind Nina's ear.

Carmen tucks her white hibiscus behind her ear. "Aren't you going to dance with Uncle Noah?"

"He should ask me himself."

Nina holds up her thin wrist to Zoe, showing off the pink watch. "Uncle Noah gave this to me."

Zoe runs her finger over the crystal face of the watch. "Your uncle loves you very much to give you something so beautiful."

Nina nods. "He's a great uncle. I'm sure he didn't ask you to dance himself because he's too scared. You know how boys are."

Zoe faces Noah, on the far side of the lawn. "Too scared, huh. Well, then, we girls must have our own strategies, mustn't we?"

Nina and Carmen giggle their enthusiastic agreement.

Zoe walks across the lawn, her high heels stabbing into the grass. She stops short in front of Noah. "That's a shameless trick, getting the girls to ask me to dance with you."

Noah flinches in surprise. "I didn't ask them to do anything."

"I don't believe you."

"I didn't ask them. I wasn't even certain you'd come today."

"Of course I would come."

Noah's gaze goes to Zoe's formfitting strapless dress, outlining the swell of her hips, the thrust of her breasts. "That's quite a dress. You can still throw a knockout punch when you want to."

"I didn't come here to throw punches."

"So, instead of punches, dance with me."

"I told you, it's over."

"I still say, it's not over until it's over. If you won't give me a last dance, let me make you a last dinner."

"Dinner! You never cooked one meal for me in our entire marriage. The only thing you did in the kitchen was open liquor bottles."

"It's an innocent invitation, a thank-you for bailing me out. If it wasn't for you and Joan, I'd still be behind bars."

"You'll be free enough when our divorce is final."

"Free, or penalized?"

Zoe studies Noah's face, looking for sincerity. Her voice softens. "Okay, dinner at your place. But understand, it is over. This will be our last dinner."

The three musicians on the bandstand stop playing. At the banquet table beneath the banyan tree, Luz clinks her champagne glass for attention. Everyone joins Luz around the table and takes a seat.

Luz's face brightens with a smile. "I cannot thank all of you enough for surrounding us with your love." She raises her glass to Nina, seated in her wheelchair between Carmen and Zoe. "Nina, you are my jewel, the bright star of Cuba shining over our family. Your gentleness and courage teach us every day a new lesson in life." Luz's throat tightens; she continues with deepening emotion. "Your strength of character nourishes the roots of our family tree for eternity." Luz raises her champagne glass higher to Nina. "A toast to you, my precious daughter, on your fifteenth birthday!"

Everyone around the table joins Luz in raising their glasses to Nina in her wheelchair. They all take a celebratory drink and cheer. Amid the cheering, Joan appears, carrying on a silver tray a three-tiered white-frosted cake. On the cake's top tier, sixteen candles, one for each year and one for good luck and growth, burn brightly. She sets the cake in front of Nina.

Nina stares wide-eyed at the cake. She looks across the candles to the other side of the table, at Luz. "Mom, can you help me blow them out?"

"Go on, honey. You can do it. This is your day."

Nina inhales deeply and concentrates. She leans down and blows. Candles on the cake flicker and go out with little puffs of smoke. One smoking candle flares up again, its wick still burning. Nina's smiling face turns to disappointment.

Zoe, next to Nina, puts her arms around her in a hug. "Brava, Nina! That last burning candle is for good luck in the future!" Nina beams as everyone applauds.

Luz holds up a gaily wrapped box. "There's one more thing. Here it is, the most exciting part of the Quince." She walks around the table and kneels next to Nina in her wheelchair. She unwraps the box. "You are becoming a woman today, so you get your first real high heels. That's the tradition—we are a very traditional people." She removes the box lid. Nina gasps at the sight of red high-heel shoes. Luz pulls off the flat white shoes Nina is wearing and slips the high heels onto her feet.

Nina throws her arms around Luz. "Mom! I love you!"

"You always wanted a pair of sparkling magic shoes like the ones Dorothy wore on her journey to see Oz. Now you'll be able to walk the Yellow Brick Road all the way to the Emerald City. When you get there and you meet Oz, tell him"—Luz bends forward and kisses Nina's forehead—"tell him how much your family adores you."

Noah, Rimbaud, and the public defender wait in the courtroom at the defendant's table. Noah keeps his eyes on the judge's empty elevated podium at the front of the room. Rimbaud's face muscles twitch. At the prosecution's table, across the aisle, three attorneys chat in low voices as they shuffle papers back and forth from their briefcases. In the back of the crowded courtroom, a tall black man wearing a suit and tie sits in the last row. His face is stern, his attention bearing straight ahead at the defendant's table.

A bailiff enters from a side door and commands loudly: "All rise. Court is in session. The Honorable Judge Helen Reese presiding." Everyone in the room rises except Rimbaud, who didn't understand what the bailiff said in English. Noah nudges Rimbaud to his feet.

The cloaked judge enters from her chambers and sits at her elevated podium. She looks down. "Be seated. Our court schedules are backed up, so time, as well as justice, is of the essence. I'll make this brief. Since the defendant's last appearance before me, I have reviewed investigative reports and detailed lab results pertinent to the murder of Pat Benson. I also perused briefs and motions from the defense counsel. I see no substantial evidence, not even circumstantial evidence, that Mr. Rimbaud Mesrine perpetuated a crime, let alone the egregious crime of murder." The judge turns her focus to the attorneys at the prosecution table. "Would the prosecution like to make a statement?"

One of the prosecution attorneys stands and answers the judge. "Your Honor, having reviewed the facts of this case, we concur with the court and see no reason to move ahead with prosecution. If it pleases the court, we accept a motion to dismiss with prejudice."

"Thank you. You may be seated." The judge turns her attention to the defendant's table. "I have consulted with federal immigration authorities regarding Mr. Mesrine's legal status. The salient fact, as presented in Mr. Mesrine's statement given voluntarily to the court interpreter, is that both his parents and three siblings were on the raft with him, headed from Haiti to América. Everyone on that raft was declared deceased upon reaching U.S. waters except for Mr. Mesrine. Since Mr. Mesrine entered the United States as an unaccompanied indigent minor, I hereby grant him political asylum and place him in the custody of his adult cousin, François Lefaille, a U.S. citizen with residence in Tampa, Florida." The judge bangs her gavel. "Case dismissed."

Rimbaud, confused, looks to Noah. His words blurt out in French: "What did she say? What's happening?"

Noah answers in French. "Political asylum. She granted you political asylum." He pulls Rimbaud up from his chair and claps him on the back.

Rimbaud looks around, still confused. He sees the tall black man walking straight down the aisle toward him. Rimbaud steps behind Noah for protection. The man stops before Noah and grabs Noah's hand in a firm grip, his voice booming in French. "I'm Cousin François Lefaille. Rimbaud's dear mother, Marie-Pierre, who died on the raft, was my aunt."

Rimbaud, hearing his mother's name, pokes his head around from behind Noah's back and stares at the man. Lefaille looks sympathetically at Rimbaud. "I left Haiti when you were just a baby. I am here for you. My dear, I am your family." Rimbaud's eyes well up with tears and he sobs. The tall man puts his arms around Rimbaud. "It's okay. You're safe now. Safe."

Noah shakes Lefaille's hand. "He'll be okay with you. Thanks."

"I thank you. The judge told me your interpretation of Rimbaud's statement helped convince her there was no legal cause to hold him."

Noah turns and bear-hugs an overwhelmed Rimbaud in an affectionate embrace. "You're free, my friend. A free man in America."

L uz stands next to the Police Chief at a lectern onstage, facing anxious reporters and a bank of television cameras. The Chief speaks into a microphone: "We have important information regarding the recent murders. Before we get started, I want to announce that the city of Key West is offering a reward of one hundred thousand dollars for information leading to the capture of the perpetrator. Detective Luz Zamora, head of the investigation, will fill you in on the latest."

Luz steps forward and adjusts the lectern microphone. A barrage of camera bulbs flash. "There are two important things we want to share with the public. The first is, we finally have images of the perpetrator. There is video taken by security cameras on the *Titan Reef* cruise ship. The second thing is, a micro–digital recorder was discovered sewn into the mouth of the *Titan Reef*'s deceased captain. After intensive lab testing, it is now confirmed that the digital recorder's brand and make match exactly the other recorders found on the bodies of two previous victims and the audio constructs of all three are executed in precisely the same manner. We will now project for you the ship's security video. At the same time, we will play the audio of the recorder discovered in the captain's mouth. We are sharing this so that any member of the public with information can step forward. Remember, there is a one-hundred-thousand-dollar reward." Luz steps away from the lectern. The room plunges into darkness.

A movie screen above the stage fills with flickering light. Images from a cruise ship's out-of-focus nighttime security camera begin to slowly take shape. The blur of a person, encased in a tight black-and-white rubber skeleton suit, becomes clear. The skeleton rappels down the massive steel hull of the ship in fluid acrobatic muscular motions by a long rope gripped in its rubber hands. A speargun is slung over its shoulder. The skeleton's grip on the rope slips; it swings erratically alongside the hull, splaying its legs and feet out, trying to get a purchase to keep from falling. The skeleton rights itself from swinging, pulls the rope taut against its chest. It hangs suspended for moments, making no move, then turns its skull face toward the camera. The face fills the entire movie screen, revealing two deep, impenetrable black eye sockets.

The reporters in the dark room gasp. Sound speakers beneath the screen blast a piercing static. From the static emerges the crackling mutant sound of an electronically altered voice.

"Look into my skeletal eyes
you who run over the Key deer
slaughter the sea turtles
erect your condominiums over natural habitats
sail on cruise ships that slash coral reefs
spew waste into pure oceans.
You shout that you are not responsible
for the earth's ills but my eternal X
cannot be escaped. I am the survivor
refusing to succumb to your polluted oceans,
smogged-up, burnt-out globe.
I am the white heron with radioactive

mud worms eating at my heart.
I rise up from the last mangrove swamp
to avenge your evil.
I am a hex doctor
a magic gangster
king of cemeteries
ultimate judge.
I am your annihilator
the great corrector.
I boogie till you bounce.
I bop till you drop.
I am Bizango."

The weird sound of Bizango's voice stops. On the movie screen, the black-and-white skeletal Bizango continues rappelling down the hull of the ship. Bizango lets go of the hanging rope. In a black-and-white blur, Bizango drops. The image of Bizango falling goes out of the movie frame. Suddenly, from another angle, a different security camera picks up Bizango's steep fall. Bizango's image becomes smaller and smaller in a seventy-five-foot plunge down the side of the hull toward the water. The white spray of a splash erupts from the water at the bottom of the hull as Bizango disappears beneath the surface. The disturbed water continues to roil, then smooths over and becomes placid.

The video on the screen ends. The bright overhead lights of the room come on. Luz steps to the lectern. She looks out at the stunned reporters. "Again, we share this information with the public so that anyone who knows anything about these heinous crimes will come forward.

We are dealing with a self-appointed ecoterrorist, killing those he thinks are responsible for killing the environment. Bizango is a ticking time bomb. He must be stopped before his next murder."

In the second-story bedroom of his dilapidated mansion, Lareck lies in bed propped up on pillows. A shawl is draped around his shoulders despite the humid night air. His sparse white hair forms a crazy unkempt halo around his head. On the nightstand beside him are scattered bottles of medications.

Noah sits next to the bed, in the old chipped wicker chair. He shakes the ice in his glass of rum and looks up to the ceiling, where a scorpion is scuttling. He watches the scorpion's hooked stinger-tail arch and twitch as it inches along. He takes a slow drink from his glass, swallows, and clears his throat. "In Key West, you have either scorpions or rats in your house. One or the other. The two will not live side by side."

Lareck's weak, watery eyes look up at the scorpion; words wheeze from his lips: "Where's Hogfish? He's supposed to be here to give me my medication. I haven't seen him for days. He couldn't care less if his old man lives or dies. I'm getting worse by the day."

Noah takes another drink, then sloshes the ice in his glass. "I wouldn't worry about Hogfish. He's probably lying low, spooked by Bizango. We're all spooked. We each fight fear in our own way. Some light a candle and pray, others have a shot of courage of one sort or another."

Lareck breaks into raspy laughter. He pushes his bed-sheet off, exposing his wrinkled and shriveled body. "Look at me. I'm already a skeleton. Maybe I'm Bizango! I'm not really trapped in this bed. I arise at night and prowl the streets in a skeleton costume. Don't you know, I'm a spook on the loose!" His raspy laugh continues, turning into a hacking cough. He falls, exhausted, back onto the bed.

Noah sets his glass on the nightstand. "I'll give you your medication. Let's not wait for Hogfish." He pours out a concoction of pills from the bottles on the nightstand and fills a glass with water from a pitcher. He puts his arm around Lareck and helps him sit up.

Lareck's hacking cough becomes louder. He takes the pills from Noah and struggles to choke them down. He swallows the pills with a groan and sputters. "Why do I keep taking these damn things to stay alive? I've already lived eighty-seven years. Doesn't seem right that I'm still hanging in when your young niece is on her way out. No matter how many pills Nina takes, she's still being pushed through the exit door. Wish I could take back half my years and give them to her." Lareck catches his breath and gives Noah a mischievous wink. "Of course, I wouldn't give Nina my best years. I wouldn't give the poor unsuspecting girl my shameless pussy-hunting years. I'm a generous man, but those years I'm keeping for myself. I'll take them to Hell with me to keep things hotter."

"There are some events in a man's life that he should only share with the devil."

"The bastard devil hasn't heard the half of it. Wait till I

get there and fill him in. He doesn't know about the Shanghai French Concession in the 1930s, before Mao finally ruined the party. My God, such antics put Toulouse-Lautrec's Paris whorehouses in the shade. I made my best paintings there. Such colorful goings-on." Lareck's wheezing breath breaks into excited hacking coughing.

Noah looks up at the ceiling. The scorpion above stops directly over Lareck. It releases its grip on the ceiling and drops, spiraling down in a fall through the air onto Lareck's bedsheet. It maneuvers its scaly body into a crawl across the sheet toward Lareck. The hooked stinger-tail vibrates, its forward clawed pincers rapidly snapping.

Noah slugs down all the rum in his glass. He scoops the scorpion up off the sheet into the empty glass. He flips the glass over onto the nightstand, trapping the scorpion inside. He watches the scorpion futilely trying to escape, clawing at the transparent walls of its prison. "Got to protect scorpions. If not, rats will take over the house. They will take over the island."

Lareck nods in agreement. "Where's my son? The rat."

Noah flips the glass right side up with the scorpion inside.

Lareck falls back onto the bed, his pale lips quivering. "Where's the rat?"

Noah quickly crosses the room with the agitated scorpion in the glass. He shoves open a window and tosses the scorpion out from the glass. The scorpion spins away.

Noah walks in the moonless night through a trash-strewn weedy lot past a battered sign barely discernible in the darkness: TROPIX PARADIZE. He continues along a row of dented and rusting mobile home trailers sitting cockeyed on concrete blocks. He stops, hesitating in front of the most dilapidated trailer. He eyes the rickety steps leading up to a closed aluminum door. Shards of feeble light shine through jagged holes in the door. He walks up the steps, careful not to slip, and bangs on the door. He waits in the silence for a response, then bangs again. From inside the trailer a jittery high-pitched male voice calls out, "No one is here! Go away!"

Noah tries the flimsy handle of the door; it is unlocked. He creaks open the door and cautiously steps inside. He looks around in dim light thrown off by one bare bulb hanging overhead from a frayed cord, its copper wires exposed. His eyes adjust to the shadowy interior. The surrounding windows are boarded over with scraps of plywood. The floor is cluttered with parts of old appliances, bent automobile hubcaps, tangled wire guts of disassembled machines, cracked baseball bats, and broken rat-traps. Seated high up on a dusty stack of yellowed newspapers in the corner is Hogfish.

Hogfish stares from beneath the bill of his fisherman's cap and shouts in a jittery voice: "I keep moving, so El Finito won't know where I am when he blows in. Got to keep moving. Got to trick Finito. How'd you find me?"

Noah opens his mouth to speak, but Hogfish jumps down from the newspapers and cuts him off. "Shut up. Don't talk. El Finito can hear you."

Noah speaks in a low voice. "I was just going to say—"

"Hey! You want an organ? Works fine!" Hogfish turns to a scratched-up wood organ shoved against the wall. He pounds his fists on the chipped black and white keys.

Noah grimaces at the screeching notes reverberating off the trailer's tin walls. He covers his ears with his hands and shouts at Hogfish, "Cut the concert!"

Hogfish stops pounding the keys; his head turns around. "You don't want the organ? You got to take something. When El Finito comes, I can't be weighed down. I've got to run. Run for my life."

"I'm here to tell you, your father doesn't have long. He wants to see you."

Hogfish holds up a dented waffle iron. "How about a waffle iron? You want a waffle iron? Everybody eats waffles."

"I don't want anything. Do you understand? Your father might die at any moment. He needs to see you."

Hogfish throws the waffle iron down with a loud clank. He kicks away boxes overflowing with trinkets and bric-a-brac, exposing on the floor an old 1950s spearfishing gun. The speargun is cocked and loaded with a sharp harpoon spear. Hogfish whips around, pointing the speargun at Noah. "You want a speargun? You can kill a shark with this."

Noah reels back. "I don't want a damn thing!"

Hogfish tosses the speargun to the floor and bangs open the top of the organ against the wall. He reaches inside the organ and pulls out a black-handled German Luger. He aims the pistol's blunt barrel muzzle at Noah. "How about a World War Two German Luger? Shoots nine-millimeter bullets. Nazis killed Yank soldiers and Jews with this!"

"What can I do with that? Shoot your El Finito when he roars ashore? Bullets can't stop a two-hundred-mile-an-hour category-five hurricane."

Hogfish moves toward Noah, frantically waving the Luger. "No one can stop El Finito except Bizango! I got a feeling about that! Got a feeling in my bones!" Hogfish stops; the Luger wobbles in his hand. "Take the gun. Shoot yourself in the head with it before Finito catches up to you. You're better off dead than to see what Finito will do. His thousand-foot tsunami will smash everyone into a million pieces of shattered bones, severed eyeballs, splintered hearts, and hurl them into space."

Noah lunges forward and grabs the barrel of the Luger, ripping it out of Hogfish's hand.

Hogfish moans and stares glassy-eyed at the junk-strewn floor. He sees his iPhone and picks it up, shoves its earbuds into his ears. He turns the volume high. His head bobs wildly to music. He lurches at Noah.

Noah whips up the Luger. "No further! Stay where you are!"

Hogfish's voice ratchets up into hysteria. "Finito's chasing you! Finito's going to get you!"

Noah backs away from Hogfish. He kicks open the closed door behind him and jumps out into the night.

The severe slant of late-afternoon sun glares off the brass instruments of a walking band of solemn men dressed in dark suits. The band plays a low-pitched funereal dirge with muted trumpets, melancholic slide trombones, and the repetitious heartrending thump of a bass drum. A long line of mourners follows the band through the open ornate iron gates of the Key West Cemetery. Directly behind the band, Luz and Noah carry a short white casket supported on their shoulders. Following the casket are Joan, Carmen, and Zoe, dressed in black, their faces grief-stricken; they support one another, arm in arm. At the very end of the procession, Hogfish pedals his rusty bicycle.

The mourners weave beneath the gray-shadowed canopy of tall palm trees. They pass between rows of tombstones and granite mausoleums littered with sun-faded plastic flowers. They finally stop before a freshly dug open grave. At the grave's head is a new white marble statue of a winged angel. The beatific angel extends in its hand above the grave a marble lily.

A somber priest, dressed in purple vestments, steps forward. His voice rises above the sound of sobbing from the mourners gathered around the grave. "Heavenly Father, we do not question Thee in Thy infinite wisdom. You have taken such a young soul to be at Your side in heaven, to seat her with the angels surrounding You. We only ask, dear Lord, that You take pity on those left behind after such an innocent has taken flight from this temporal world. Guide the family and all her loved ones through this storm of anguish. Give us each the faith and courage to survive what seems an unjust and overbearing sorrow."

Carmen cries out in a wail of pain; her body slumps; she is held up by Joan and Zoe.

Luz and Noah lower the casket on velvet ropes to the grave's bottom. Only muffled sobbing is heard as the casket descends and settles onto the hard earth.

Carmen, her face wet with tears, her knees shaking, steps next to Luz and hands her a box. Luz opens the box and pulls out a pair of red high-heel shoes. She steps to the edge of the grave and lets the shoes slip from her fingers and drop down. She looks at the shoes glittering next to the white-enameled casket. "Here are your magic shoes, my darling Nina. When you get to the end of the Yellow Brick Road, tell Oz what I told you. Tell him that your family adores you." From Luz's eyes, tears spiral downward into the open grave, onto the red shoes.

A line of slump-shouldered mourners, their heads bowed, files out between the iron cemetery gates. In a far, hidden corner of the cemetery, only Hogfish is left. He stands astride his rusty bicycle with its line of barbed J-hooks strung between the handlebars. He watches the entrance gates to make certain no one is coming back. He jams the earbuds of his iPhone into his ears and jumps up onto his bicycle's cracked leather seat. He pedals furiously, swerving the bike on a snaking path among the gravestones. He hits the brakes and skids to a stop in front of Nina's grave. The grave is filled in with dirt, its top covered with bouquets of flowers tied by colorful satin ribbons. The fragrance of the flowers is a heady perfume mix in the shifting breeze.

Hogfish gazes across the grave to the winged stone angel extending a marble lily. The angel's smoothly chiseled face is serene.

Hogfish jabs his finger at the angel. His shouting voice echoes across the cemetery. "Smell the air! When El Finito comes, the air is filled with the stink of dead turtles! Feel his filthy weather creeping up your back. Oppressive weather! Weather that's hot and calculating! Wants to explode in your face! To annihilate you!"

Hogfish turns away from the angel. He grips the bicycle's metal handlebars in a white-knuckle hold. He shakes the handlebars, rattling loudly the line of dangling J-hooks. His chest heaves, he struggles for breath, he sucks in air deeply. He looks back in anguish at the angel, tears streaming from his eyes. "Don't let Finito steal Nina out of her grave! Finito's almost here!"

The circular steps inside the Key West Lighthouse spiral up in a steep rise of eighty-six feet above Noah. He climbs the steps in the hot, confined air and stops at the uppermost landing to catch his breath. He steps through a narrow passageway leading outside onto an iron catwalk suspended around the top of the light-house. He follows the catwalk beneath a massive glass light beacon above. He stops. Before him is Luz.

Luz stands with her hands gripping the top railing of the catwalk. She stares out over the view of the island city's tightly packed tin-roofed houses melding into the blue of the surrounding ocean. She is startled by Noah's words coming from behind her.

"Joan told me I might find you here. She said this is where you come when you want to be alone."

Luz remains silent, not releasing her tight grip on the railing, her breathing labored.

Noah takes a step back. "Maybe I shouldn't have come. I understand. I can leave you alone if you want."

Luz keeps her sight on the sweeping vista. "My father used to bring me up here when I was a little girl. He told me that when this was first lit, in the 1840s, doves flying here over the ocean from Cuba mistook the brilliant light for the sun. The doves flew straight into the beacon." Luz turns slowly to Noah, her eyes filled with suffering. "That species of dove that crashed to their deaths against this beacon is now extinct. Those doves will never be on this earth again. Gone forever, like my Nina."

Noah looks at Luz, seeking a way out of the sadness. "You still have two doves to live for. Carmen and Joan are waiting for you. You are needed at home."

Luz turns away. Her gaze goes back to the vista of the island and the blue horizon beyond.

Lareck lies in bed, listless, near death. His watery eyes stare up at the ceiling. He rasps for breath with an open mouth. A white sheet covers his body up to the neck. A scorpion scuttles along the white sheet, its front pincer claws clicking.

In the wicker chair next to the bed, Hogfish rocks his body back and forth to music blasting through his iPhone's earbuds.

The scorpion slithers up the bedsheet onto Lareck's neck. The creature creeps up the side of Lareck's cheek toward his open mouth. He struggles to speak as he looks pleadingly at Hogfish, his words barely audible. "Scor . . . pions. Scorpions or . . . rats. Got to choose. Make your . . . choice."

Hogfish bobs his head to the music, watching the scorpion progress up Lareck's cheek. He reaches out his hand and clamps it tight over Lareck's mouth. Lareck's eyes widen in fear, his breath cut.

The scorpion crawls onto the back of Hogfish's hand covering Lareck's mouth. Hogfish raises his hand close to his face and stares into the scorpion's amber eyes. The scorpion stares back; its front scissored pincers widen to attack; its arched stinger-tail vibrates to sting. Hogfish flicks his hand, knocking the scorpion to the floor. He jumps up and stomps the heel of his shoe down, crushing the scorpion's body and squishing out a snot-colored slime of innards.

Hogfish shouts at the terrified Lareck. "The air will stink of dead scorpions and rats when El Finito turns the world upside down! Fish will be thrown up into the sky!

Pelicans will rain down. Iguanas will explode! Finito is coming to end it all!"

Luxury cars are parked in front of a sprawling red-roofed Mediterranean-style villa. Behind the villa, bright overhead lights shine down on a tennis court where two pit bulls ferociously tear into each other's flesh. Circled around the dogs, betting men shout for blood. Prominent among the men, in his tight Italian silk suit and shiny alligator shoes, is Hard Puppy. At his side are two meth-tweaked party girls, one white and one black, both wearing skintight dresses and stiletto high heels. The party girls shriek as one of the pit bulls rips the throat out of the other in a spray of blood.

Hard pumps his fist triumphantly in the air, then slaps the asses of the party girls. The men around Hard groan with disappointment as he boasts with flashing platinum teeth.

"My bitch won big bucks! She be like a hyena! My bitch can tear the asshole out of a fleein' zebra!"

Beneath a full moon, Hard Puppy's black SUV speeds on the Seven Mile Bridge. The bridge spans sixty-five feet above the ocean in a concrete blade crossing over the deep channel between the Gulf of Mexico and the Florida Strait, linking the Upper Keys to the lower islands. Silhouetted in the moon's glow alongside the bridge is the forlorn remnant of the old Overseas Railroad, blown away to its stubby concrete trestles during the 1935 hurricane that dumped four hundred men to their deaths in the shark-infested waters. Hard glances over at the old bridge and gives an appreciative whistle through his platinum teeth. High on meth and pumped on adrenaline, he steers the SUV ahead with jerky aggressiveness while singing along to the radio's bass-beat thump of angry rap music booming from surround-sound speakers.

On the front seat, next to Hard, the white party girl sits with her skinny ass rooted into the lap of the black girl. They both lean in next to Hard. Behind them, in the back cargo cab, the winning pit bull paces in an iron-barred cage. The dog's stout body is ripped and bleeding from its recent fight.

Hard shouts to the party girls above the rap music. "To men I give shit! To ladies I give favors!" He grabs the plump silicone breast of the white girl through her dress. She launches into shrill giggling. The caged pit bull in the back pricks up its ears to the sound and growls with deep-throated menace. Hard punches the SUV's accelerator pedal to the floor, speeding the SUV to the end of the bridge and onto a narrow road with mangrove swamps pressed up against it on both sides. The rap music blasts, the pit bull growls. Hard turns down the volume on the radio. "This be bad music I be playin'. But I got badder. I can sing Civil War times bad ass."

The girls shout encouragement. "Sing it, Hard!"

Hard snaps his fingers with loud cracks, giving himself the musical beat. He throws back his head and opens his mouth, his teeth glistening to the words of the song.

"Goin' to run all de night.
Goin' to run all de day.
Bet me money on a bobtailed nag.
Somebody be bettin' de gray.
Oh! De doo-da day!"

Hard bangs his fist on the steering wheel. "Now, that be bad-ass nigga! It be written by a runaway slave."

The white girl screws her face into a perplexed expression. "That's not a black song. That was written by some white dude. I learned about it in high school."

Hard backhands the white girl, one of the flashing gold rings on his fingers cutting a gash into her face.

"Girl! Don't you be messin' with nigga music! You know nothin' 'bout nigga!"

The girl's hand flies up to the blood gushing from her cheek. She screams in panic. The pit bull in the back sniffs blood and howls. Hard guns the SUV.

Several miles ahead of Hard Puppy's SUV, the narrow road curves into a pine-tree forest. Out of the forest, a Key deer emerges. The deer's thin, graceful body is coated with apricot-and-fawn-colored fur, its short white tail stiffly upright. The deer sniffs the air for danger and waits. Other Key deer emerge from the pine trees; they follow the lead deer alongside the empty road to a patch of grass growing next to the asphalt. The deer graze on the grass, their noses down alongside the edge of the road.

The tranquil night silence around the Key deer is broken by the rocketing whine from the SUV's four-hundred-horsepower engine firing off on its V-8 cylinders. The deer stop grazing and look up. The SUV careens around the corner of the road into sight, the harsh rush of its large tires racing over asphalt. The deer bolt and scatter into the trees. One confused deer stays behind, frozen with fear in the center of the road. The three-ton SUV smashes into the deer. The small body catapults forward through the air.

The SUV's wide tires burn to a stop. Hard stumbles out of the vehicle into the beams of its halogen headlights. He squints at what the bright beams illuminate. Lying twenty feet ahead, on black asphalt, is the bleeding body of the deer. He turns away from the animal and kneels in front of the SUV's crosshatch chrome grille. He runs his finger below the grille, along a dent in the thick bumper. He looks back angrily at the deer lying on the blacktop. "You little midget shit! Should be locked in a zoo! Messed with my ride!"

A high-pitched, eerie whistling comes from the pine forest at the edge of the highway. Hard's head snaps around. He looks belligerently into the trees, shouting toward the sound. "They be more of you midget fuckers in there? Come on out! I'll put my pit bull on you! She chase you down and chew your asshole out!"

The strange, eerie whistling stops. Hard sees no movement among the trees. He shrugs his shoulders impatiently and climbs back into the SUV. He slams the door and rolls down his driver's-side window. He cocks his head out the open window to listen. He hears nothing. He rolls up his window and restarts the SUV.

Next to Hard, the two party girls stare wide-eyed through the windshield at an apparition emerging from the dark forest. The girls shudder and lock their arms tightly around each other. Hard sees the apparition. His words spit out in surprise: "Fuck me! What be him?"

Walking out of the forest into the SUV's headlights is the Bizango skeleton, encased in tight rubber and skull mask. Bizango stops in the center of the road and holds up a speargun loaded with a sharp, cocked spear.

Inside the SUV's back cab, the pit bull sees the black-and-white skeleton. The dog's deep, murderous bark reverberates in the cab as it hurls its body against the iron cage bars, thrashing to break through and attack Bizango.

The girls scream hysterically. Hard shouts above the screaming and barking: "Everybody shut up!" He glares at Bizango through the windshield. "Don't mess with me, mo-fo! You be doomed! Time to let the dog out!"

Hard jumps from the SUV and runs around to the rear hatch door; he yanks the door open. The pit bull—inside its cage, behind bars—howls at Hard to be freed. Hard unlatches the cage's steel lock and swings the door back. "Go, you hyena! Rip his asshole out!"

The snarling pit bull leaps from its cage, knocking Hard aside. The dog hits the outside pavement running, its clawed paws digging in as it propels its muscular body upward and hurls furiously through the air at the skeleton standing in the middle of the road.

Bizango whips up the speargun, aims, and pulls the trigger. The gun's C2 cartridge fires in a whoosh. The spear springs free in a blurred trajectory, its flight meeting the opposite rush of the dog in midair. The spear pierces with a crunching thwack into the bone bulge of the dog's rib cage. The dog howls, but its body keeps hurling forward through the air at Bizango. The dog's weight falls from the air, drops with a bouncing thud at the skeleton's feet. Bizango looks down at the dog, its barrel-shaped body inert, its bloodied tongue hanging out onto the asphalt, its startled, dying eyes staring up. Bizango reaches down and rips out the bloody spear from the dog's rib cage.

Hard jumps back into the SUV's driver's seat. He peers through the windshield at Bizango outside and grits his platinum teeth. "You killed my bitch! Nobody lives who kills my bitch!" He grips the steering wheel tight with both hands, jams his foot to the floor on the accelerator pedal, and yells above the whining engine, "Motherfuckin' spook! You die!"

The SUV roars straight toward the skeleton. Bizango quickly reloads the gun with the bloody spear and reels back from the SUV as it speeds by, just an inch away, in a rush of wind. Bizango fires the gun. The spear shatters the glass of the driver's-side window. It flies right behind Hard's head and smashes out the window on the opposite side of the cab. The SUV keeps going. The snarl from its engine fades away into silence.

Bizango walks to the small deer lying on the blacktop. The deer gasps for breath; its eyes bulge. Bizango's black rubber fingers wipe blood away from the deer's nostrils. Its body jolts with a life-releasing electric shock, then becomes deathly still.

Bizango stares at the deer. From the surrounding forest, a throb of insects starts, crickets chirp, frogs croak. Bizango gently lifts up the deer in skeleton arms. Bizango's masked skull head swivels up to the sky as the dead body is raised toward the stars above.

Cackling bantam chickens scratch and peck in the dust outside the front door of a flimsy boarded shack beaten gray by weather and time. The chickens scatter as Noah walks between them and up the steps. The shack's door is open; inside the shadowy depths sits a dark-skinned African-Cuban woman wearing a flowing white cotton dress. The bones of her nearly century-old body are twig-thin, and her small skull is pulled tight with wrinkled skin. She rocks back and forth in a creaky chair as she fans herself with a folded magazine in the stifling heat. She calls out to Noah from the shadows, "Comes ins. I bees 'spectin' you."

Noah steps out of the sun into near darkness and stands awkwardly. "How did you know I was coming?"

"All de mins, dey comin' to Auntie sooner de betters. Dey gots de dollar problems, dey gots de love problems. An' ol' Auntie, she's 'bout fixin' de cure. Nothin' Auntie cain't fix, from an emptied wallet to a bustin' heart. I sees yo got de womins problems. Dat's why yo comin' to me."

Noah pulls his pint bottle of rum from his frayed coat pocket and takes a swig, then wipes his lips. He stays silent. He slips the pint back into his pocket.

Auntie waves her hand around the cramped room. Faded photographs of black saints torn from faith-healing magazines are tacked to the walls. The rafters are hung with bundles of dried herbs and flowers of every type, color, and scent. The countertops are piled with tins containing exotic powders, oils, and extracts. Dusty glass jars are filled with bent coins and rusted nails. Auntie claps her age-polished white palms together and stops rocking in her chair. She pushes up on an ebony cane toward Noah. "I be knowin' 'bout womins makin' de mins cry! Yo come runnin' to me's cryin' like de lost boy." She pulls a matchstick out of a box and strikes it; the flame flares. She lights a votive candle inside a red jar with the image of a Black Virgin painted on the glass. She hands the jar to Noah. "Hold dis tight."

Noah grips the jar. Auntie studies his illuminated face in the glow of the burning candle. Her trembling bony hand comes up and feels the contours of his face. She shakes her head; her stringy white hair covers her face as she speaks. "Yo mighty bad. Yo gots only de one womin in life to loves. Dat womin bees runnin' away hard. Yo never goin' catch her 'less yo listens to de Auntie."

"I hope it isn't going to be expensive to win the race."

"What bees de price of love?"

Noah sets down the votive jar and takes from his pocket a crisp one-hundred-dollar bill. "I heard around town that you could help me win the race."

Auntie pushes the offered money away. "Put dat debil green paper back in yo pocket. Where I bees headed, dey don' take dats. Dey takes only de pure of de hearts."

Noah slips the bill back into his pocket and pulls out the rum bottle. He takes a swallow as he watches Auntie hobble around the room on her cane.

Auntie unhooks from the wall a straw basket hanging from a nail. She takes the basket to a tall cupboard and opens its door, exposing shelves rowed with glass vials filled with leaves and petals of crushed and ground plants and flowers. She pulls vials out, uncorking each and sniffing it, her nostrils twitching at the heady aromas. She recorks all the vials and packs them in the basket. She hobbles back to Noah and hands him the basket with a knowing wink. "Dese will wins back yo true love." Her eyes glow with pride at the glass vials in the basket. She taps each vial's corked top as she explains their ingredients: "Dis one bees de ginger root to entice her. Here bees dried strawberries to unlock her secrets. Of course, passionflower to soften de heart, and verbena oil to bees keepin' her loves."

"How can I win the race with this stuff?"

"Yo gots to trust de Auntie. Puts verbena oil in her water glass. Strawberries in de soup. Ginger root on de fish. Passionflower in her dessert."

"That's everything? You sure you didn't leave anything out?"

"Dese will do de trick. Only one mo' thing."

"Tell me."

Auntie hobbles over to a carved chest and creaks open its heavy lid. She pulls out a small purple velvet bag and smiles at Noah. "If yo gets close enough to her, rub dis on her earlobes. She bees a juicy peach for de pickin'."

"You don't know my Zoe. Right now she's more of a hard pit than a soft fruit." Noah takes the velvet bag and feels its weight. "What's inside?"

"Rare in de natures. Royal jelly from de Brazilian queen bee."

"This is my last chance before my wife becomes my ex-wife." Noah pockets the bag. "I can't thank you enough."

"No needs de thanks, only de belief. But de magics don' works 'less yo gives up dat demon rum in a bottle yo suckin' on all de day long like a starvin' babies pulled from de mommies' teet. Alcohol bees de magics-killer. Dat demon goin' pull you all de ways down into de hells."

The outdoor food market is crowded with island locals and tourists jostling one another between open-air stalls piled with vivid mounds of tropical fruits and vegetables. Noah stops before one of the stalls and chooses from the exotic selection of purple plantain bananas, brown tamarind, yellow egg-fruit, orange loquat, blue-speckled mangoes, and green sweetsop. He moves on to a stall with a palm-thatched roof, protecting it from the overhead sun, where fresh sea fare is sprawled across iced trays. He studies the wet display of octopus, crab, horse conch, tuna, shark, dolphinfish, grouper, stingray, and snapper. He pokes a finger against an open-mouthed black grouper, then jabs a fat red snapper.

The stall's monger, gripping a curved-blade gutting knife in his hand and wearing a white rubber apron streaked with fish blood, suspiciously watches Noah poking the fish. The monger shouts with gruff irritation: "Why you pokin' that snapper? You gonna eat it . . . or you gonna make love to it?"

"Both."

"Then, buddy, that's not the one for you." The monger looks over the colorful fish arrayed on the iced trays. He slaps the bright scales of a yellowfin tuna. "Here's the one. She's got a firm body and clear eyes."

"I'll take her."

On the Gulf side of Key West, known as Land's End, where once shrimping, fishing, and turtling boats were docked years before, are anchored tourist sunset cruise and glass-bottom boats, elaborate yachts, and fancy sailboats. Facing this leisure-time fleet is an open-sided restaurant serving buckets of peel-your-own shrimp and platters of shell-shucked gritty oysters. At the edge of the farthest dock is a long wooden shed where shark bodies by the hundreds were once piled before being reduced to fillet slabs, severed fins, and skins. The shed is now filled with a selection of souvenir postcards,

T-shirts, seashell necklaces, suntan lotion, and plastic sandals. To the side of the shed is a concrete saltwater holding pen. The deep-water pen is the last of the turtle kraals constructed in the 1890s, where captured turtles were dumped by the boatload from docked schooners to be slaughtered for steaks, soup, combs, and toothbrush handles.

At the top edge of the concrete pen, Luz stands staring down into the water. She watches trapped snook and barracuda kept as a tourist attraction. The fish dart back and forth in silver flashes, searching for a way out.

The Chief comes up behind Luz and stands alongside her. He hands over a thick manila envelope. "Here it is, promised I'd get it. I've got pull with the boys in a state-of-the-art Miami lab. Told them it was for an important case when I sent the blood samples. They fast-tracked it through."

"I suppose I should say thanks, but I don't know what it says." Luz takes the envelope. "Have you read it?"

"I wouldn't know how to read it—too technical, cutting-edge DNA-predisposition genetic stuff. Only a few labs in the country can do this. It's what you wanted."

"You don't have such a happy face. Did they tell you what it says?"

"Of course they told me." The Chief looks down at the circling fish in the water. "I don't know how I'd react if I got this news. Jump off a bridge maybe, stay at home twenty-four/seven with my family, go up on a mountaintop to meditate, or shoot heroin."

Luz scrapes her fingernails across the thick envelope, cutting into the paper.

The Chief looks back at her. "I hate to say this, but,

because of how the testing worked out, you should quit the force."

"Never."

"Go home and be with Carmen and Joan."

"No, they would know why I was there, just sitting around the house. It's better if life goes on, and they are strong with that. It's too much for them to bear after what happened to Nina. They couldn't go through it. They'd be crushed."

"Given this new information, I could ask for your resignation. This can jeopardize your job performance. You're still fit now, but any day that could change."

"I won't quit while Bizango is still out there."

"I'll make you a deal. Stay on until Bizango is caught, then go home to your family."

Luz turns and gives the Chief a firm handshake. "It's a deal. I can live with that."

"It has to be. I can't take the chance of keeping you on."

Luz peers down into the pen; she sees her own reflection on the water's surface above the snook and barracuda making their futile runs at freedom. "I used to come here after school as a kid. Back then they kept a six-hundred-seventy-five-pound loggerhead turtle in this pen. He was a hundred thirty-nine years old, and famous for biting off the fingers of the turtle hunters who captured him in the ocean. Big George, they called him. He was a celebrity, a real tourist attraction, the biggest turtle in the world in captivity. Every day I'd throw a head of lettuce into the water for George. George would circle around the pen, then cut above the surface and give a big blow of water as he went for the floating lettuce. George wasn't a meat eater. He loved lettuce."

The Chief stands closer to Luz, his shoulder touching hers. "The DNA results I brought you don't lie. You don't have much time left. You already knew your breast cancer came back, but this test turned up two different kinds of cancer waiting to spread. You've got a deadly trifecta going. I just want you to understand: should you change your mind and decide to walk away from the force now, no one will say you didn't serve honorably. In fact, everyone will say how brave you were to hang in so long."

Luz doesn't look up from the water. "I remember the day George died. When he gasped his last breath in this pen, he was slaughtered and made into soup and combs. I was inconsolable. I cried myself to sleep every night after. My dad gave me five dollars to go buy myself something to cheer me up. I went to the Catholic church—they have a grotto there with a life-size Virgin statue inside. You can pay money to light a candle for the Virgin to protect you from hurricanes, or answer your prayers. With the five bucks, I lit up all the candles in the grotto for Big George."

The Chief turns away from the pen and steps back. He pulls out his wallet and takes out a five-dollar bill. "What do you say"—he holds up the bill with a grin—"we go to the grotto and light us some candles."

Zoe sits at Noah's kitchen table, wearing a bare-shouldered halter-top sundress. Her blond hair is swept up in a French knot, exposing diamond-stud earrings in her lobes. She watches with fascination as Noah works at the stove over pots and pans of steaming and frying food. "When did you take up cooking?"

Noah carefully flips two yellowfin-tuna fillets simmering in a pan over a gas flame. "I've only recently become interested in the alchemy of the culinary arts." He uncorks a glass vial and spreads crushed ginger root on the fish. He opens the oven door and sprinkles passionflower petals onto a baking plantain-banana pie.

"'Alchemy of the culinary arts'? You make it sound like something exotic. Women cook every day. No big deal." She picks up the water glass in front of her and takes a sip. Her mouth puckers. "This water tastes like it's got bitter lemon in it or something."

"Do you like it?"

Zoe smacks her lips. "It's tangy. I don't know if I like it or not."

"Would you like something more than water?"

"Like some rum, maybe?"

"That's not what I meant. I'm just trying to be a good husband."

"A good husband? Too late for that. I gave you every chance a woman can give. I brought the final divorce document with me. All you have to do is sign it."

Noah opens the refrigerator door and takes out a bowl of strawberry soup. "At least we can have dinner; here's the first course." He places the bowl in front of her and sits close.

"What a weird-looking soup." She bends her head and sniffs at the pink concoction with red nuggets of dried strawberries floating on top.

Noah scoops a spoonful of soup from the bowl and holds it up to her lips.

Zoe laughs nervously. "I'm not sure I want this. What do you know about cooking, anyway?"

"There's only one way to find out. Close your eyes and take a sip."

She doesn't close her eyes.

"Trust me."

Zoe reluctantly shuts her eyes. Noah moves the spoon near her parting lips. He slides the spoon into her mouth, spilling a trickle of soup onto her lips. She keeps her eyes closed as she swallows. Her lips glisten a bright strawberry-pink. He places his hand under her chin, turning her face up to kiss her.

Her eyes open. "It's delicious! What bizarre stuff did you put in this? I want the recipe!"

"Only strawberries and sugar."

She licks the red residue off her lips. "No, I taste something else."

"I put my love in it. All my love."

Zoe flinches at the sudden intimacy. She looks at the empty rum bottle in the center of the table. A burning candle is stuck in the bottle's narrow neck.

Noah touches one of the bright stones on her earlobe. "These are the earrings I gave you on our wedding day."

"Don't get any ideas. I just wore them because they go with this dress."

"And I bought you that dress for our first wedding anniversary. It still fits you like a silk glove."

"I told you not to get any ideas." She stares at the empty rum bottle in the center of the table. Inside the bottle, at its bottom, is her gold wedding ring. "I see my ring is exactly where it was when I was here the last time."

"There's a prize in each and every bottle of rum."

She looks back at him. "You haven't been drinking tonight. Why?"

"I stopped. Trying to walk the sober trail."

"Famous first words."

"I quit for you."

"Famous last words. We'll see how long that lasts."

They fall into silence, watching the candle in the bottle burn. The ring inside the bottle shines.

He shifts his gaze back to her earrings. "I think your diamonds have lost their sparkle."

She pats her ears. "Really? I think they still look good."

"They aren't as lustrous as when I first gave them to you. Someone told me that the only way to bring back the original sparkle of diamonds is to rub royal jelly from the Brazilian queen bee on them."

"And I'll bet Mr. Alchemist the Cook has some of that jelly stuff around here somewhere, don't you?"

Noah slips from his coat pocket a purple velvet bag. He unties the bag and pulls out a corked glass vial containing honey-colored jelly. He opens the vial and dips a finger into the jelly. He rubs the jelly onto one of her diamond earrings, then massages the slick substance into the soft skin of her surrounding earlobe.

Her words come with intimate breathiness. "Are they sparkling yet?"

He leans close to her, his lips almost touching hers as he whispers, "Sparkling, like the sun. Radiant, like you."

Zoe pulls back and stands. She grabs her purse from a chair and snaps it open, taking out a bundled stack of papers. She slaps the bundle on the table. "I said this would be our last dinner."

"But you only tasted the soup."

"No more games. Sign the divorce papers." She turns to leave.

Noah leaps up and grabs her arm. "Wait, I'll walk you home."

"Walk me home? I don't need you to walk me home. I'm a big girl."

"It's dark outside. There's a killer on the loose."

"A killer on the loose?" She stares into Noah's eyes with a sudden illumination. "It's you, isn't it? You've been the one following me home at night after I close up the bar."

"Of course it was me. I told you, it's not safe."

"I don't need a knight on a white horse to protect me! I just need a sober man who believes in himself and is one hundred percent present!" She spins around and walks out.

Noah slumps back down on the chair at the table. His lips turn down as he looks at the stack of divorce papers. His fingers drum lightly on the papers, then drum harder and harder. His hands begin shaking uncontrollably. He shoves his chair back with a loud scrape against the floor. He turns the flame off beneath the pan of burning fish. He yanks open a cupboard and pulls out a full bottle of rum. He opens the bottle and tilts it toward his mouth; the glass tip of the bottle touches his trembling lips. He turns swiftly, holding the bottle upside down over the sink next to him. He watches the dark rum flow down the sink drain and disappear. He stares at the empty bottle with a look of shocked remorse. "Goddamn, that was stupid!" He grabs the hard edge of the sink, his knuckles white against the porcelain as he holds on. "But I've got to try!" His body begins shaking violently as he fights against the barbed blood rush of alcohol deprivation consuming him.

Luz drives her white Charger slowly along Duval Street. She keeps a vigilant watch on the tourists and locals navigating their way along the crowded, hot sidewalk in the humidity of the high-noon day. A police dispatcher's voice crackles from the car's radio speaker.

"Alpha-zero-zero-eight. Respond to Code Five at Blue Hole Key Deer Refuge on Big Pine Key!"

Luz wheels her car around with the siren wailing and heads down a narrow side alley. At the end of the alley, Hogfish appears, pedaling his bicycle directly at the car. Luz stomps on the brakes; the car skids, its front bumper stopping just before smashing into Hogfish.

Hogfish rises up on the cracked leather seat of his bicycle. He points his bony finger at Luz and shouts above her car's siren: "The statue angel guarding Nina's grave will protect her! El Finito won't be able to dig up Nina and violate her when his devil's breath blows this island to hell!" Hogfish slams his butt back down on the bicycle seat. "Almost Halloween! Finito's almost here!" He pedals away in a manic fury.

Luz revs her Charger's engine and drives off, quickly leaving behind Key West's narrow streets. The red outside lights of her car flash as she speeds north on the broad concrete ribbon of the Overseas Highway, skimming above the vast ocean. She crosses over a series of bridges linking the highway from island to island. On one side of the highway suddenly looms a billboard announcing ENTERING NATIONAL KEY DEER REFUGE. Luz wheels the Charger into a hard turn after the sign and travels a gravel road into a pine-tree forest. Her car bumps along the road, kicking up a stream of dust. The gravel road abruptly dead-ends. A dirt trail is ahead, leading deeper into the forest. Blocking the trail is a row of parked police cars. She slows her Charger and cuts the engine.

Moxel stands in front of his squad car, his beefy arms crossed tightly over his broad chest. He bends down and peers at Luz through her car window. "You won't believe what's at the Blue Hole. I'm the one who found it. Already got law enforcement from half the county here."

Luz swings her door open and steps out, knocking Moxel back. "You're a hero. Always the first one to bag the big stuff. Why wasn't I called in earlier?"

"No reason for you to have rushed. We're miles away from Key West jurisdiction. We're in County Sheriff territory."

"What did you find?"

Moxel fires a sharp spit at the dirt trail. "Why don't you just trot along to have a peeky-poo for yourself."

Luz follows the trail as it twists through tall, spindly trees. She comes to the end of the trail, where the forest abruptly opens up into a vast clearing. Before her is the Blue Hole, a lake of intense bright-blue water filling the depths of a former coral-rock quarry. The pathway to the Blue Hole is blocked by stretched yellow crime-scene tape. On the far side of the tape, forensic investigators, dressed in white jumpsuits and wearing white latex gloves, scour the area.

Standing at the shoreline of the Blue Hole, the Key West Police Chief and the uniformed County Sheriff converse intensely with a police diver who wears a swimsuit, face mask, and rubber foot flippers, and holds a long pole with a cloth net attached to its tip. He nods to the Chief and Sheriff, then wades into the Blue Hole's water up to his shoulders. He swims out to the center of the Hole, holding the long pole in one hand above his head. He treads water, lowers the pole, and skims the net across the water's surface toward a round floating object. He scoops up the object with the net and swims back toward the shore.

The Chief spots Luz standing behind the stretched yellow tape. He walks to her and lifts the tape, beckoning her to step through. "You're going to be surprised what Moxel found floating in the Hole this morning."

Luz steps under the tape. "What was Moxel doing here?"

"Fishing. Some big ones in these waters if the gators don't get them first. Place is crawling with gators."

"Why was I called in so late?"

"I told Moxel to have you radio-dispatched right away, an hour ago. This ties into our investigation."

"Moxel waited. I just got the call."

"Forget it. Come with me."

Luz follows the Chief to the Blue Hole. The diver emerges from the water onto the muddy shore, holding the long pole; inside the dripping net is the severed head of Hard Puppy, his face lacerated with crisscrossed purple gashes, his eyes plucked out, and his ears slashed off.

Luz exhales with surprise. "Looks like he was attacked by his own pit bulls. They chewed his head off."

The Chief nods at Hard's lips, sewn crudely shut with fishing line. "Pit bulls can't do that. That's Bizango. Bizango fed Hard to the gators."

"Can't know the gators ate him until the forensics come in."

The Chief slips off a pair of binoculars slung around his neck on a leather strap. He hands the binoculars to Luz and points across the Blue Hole to the opposite shore. "Check out that bad-ass scene over there."

Luz looks through the lenses. Across the water, on the far shore, she sees three twelve-foot green-scaled alligators bellied in the mud. The alligators' nostrils are flared; the jaws of their snouted mouths gape open, exposing long rows of razor-sharp teeth.

The Chief prods Luz. "It gets worse. Look above the gators."

Luz raises the binoculars and refocuses beyond the alligators on the muddy bank. She spots a lone pine tree. The brittle bark of the tree's trunk is spray-painted with a red **X**. From the center of the **X** protrudes a steel spear shining in the sunlight.

A sleek seventy-foot-long sport-fishing boat plows through the water at twenty knots. Big Conch is strapped by a leather shoulder harness into a teakwood marlin-fighting chair on the boat's aft deck. His bare, broad chest strains against the leather straps as he leans into the bow of his fourteen-foot-long fishing rod, its line spinning out from the reel. Big's line runs farther out into the white-water wake left behind the boat's diesel-engine thrust. With the rod's butt anchored in the fighting chair's steel gimbal between his legs, he reels hard to recapture the line. The muscles of his arms bulge and sweat breaks out on his face. The tip of the pole curves and bends almost double, on the verge of breaking.

The boat's first mate stands behind Big in the fighting chair. The mate whoops with appreciation at Big's skill, urging him on. "You got her now!"

Big bellows at the mate, "How many runs am I up to?"

"Over twenty! She's been running in and out for the last three hours!"

Big presses his chest forward against the leather harness as the bent pole's line whirs back out. Diesel-exhaust smoke clouds up around him from the boat's engines' backing down into reverse to follow the running marlin.

The mate shouts, "Don't buck the reel! Let her take the line or you'll snap the rod!"

Big hollers above the reel's screech, "Shut up, asshole! Don't tell me the obvious!"

Behind the boat, the roiling water parts and a massive blue marlin sails high into the air. The marlin's muscular body twists for freedom in a mighty shake against the barbed hook sunk deep into its bill. The fish lurches its full body upright, trying to throw the line, its long bill pointed skyward as it tail-dances in skipping leaps over the surface of the ocean.

The mate whoops at the top of his lungs. "Look at that! She's a record breaker!"

The marlin dives out of sight.

Big reels back quickly on the line's sudden slack. "That was her last run! She's gotta be played out! I'm bringing her in! Get the gaff!"

The mate grabs a long steel gaff with a snarl hook at its end. He leans over the transom with the gaff, eager for action.

Big Conch's sport-fishing boat cuts a wide wake through the surface of the water. From atop its twenty-five-foot-high aluminum crow's-nest lookout, a cloth pennant rips in the hot wind. On the white pennant is the black image of a marlin. Big stands in the cockpit of his boat with the mahogany-wood helm gripped in his hands. The mate works on the bloodied deck, lashing down the giant fish.

Ahead of Big's boat, a floating dark speck appears on the horizon. Big turns his mahogany helm, steering toward the speck. The speck grows larger, finally coming into full view. It is a thirty-six-foot West Indian Heritage trawler with a radio-transmitter antenna bolted to its deck. The trawler is silhouetted against the sky, its name across the hull, *Noah's Lark.* Big slows his boat.

Inside the trawler's pilothouse, Noah looks through the window at the sport-fishing boat with Big at the helm. He idles his engine and goes outside onto the deck.

Big bellows across the water at Noah: "Hey, pirate! You've lost your treasure! Heard Zoe's divorcing you for good!" He laughs and throttles up his fourteen-hundred-horsepower engines with a guttural diesel roar. His boat speeds into a tight circle around Noah.

Noah's trawler rocks from the high wakes roiled by the larger boat. The trawler violently lists to its side, slamming Noah to the deck. A wave crashes over him, washing him to the deck's edge. He reaches out and grabs the steel strut of the radio-transmitter antenna to keep from being swept overboard.

Big circles his speeding boat closer, causing higher-curling waves to smash against the trawler's hull.

The trawler rolls up, then lurches low, tipping into a near-capsizing slant. Noah clings to the radio tower with one hand. He raises his other hand and stiffens his middle finger at Big. His voice soars above the roar of Big's engines: "Fuck you!"

Big's voice booms back: "Truth Dog! Sink to the bottom of the sea! Maybe you'll find your dick down there!"

Noah opens his mouth to shout back but chokes on an incoming wave of seawater. He coughs hard, gasping desperately for air, as he hangs on to the tower for his life.

Along Key West's sport-fishing pier, boats are tied up in a row. At the end of the pier, Big and his mate stand with a crowd of sunburnt fishermen. The men watch with anticipation as Big's huge blue marlin is hoisted by a pulley chain hanging from an iron weighing scale.

A craggy old fisherman wearing fish-gut-stained khaki trousers and a frayed long-billed cap comes up next to Big and nudges him. "Hey, fella, what'd you hit her with?"

Big keeps his eyes on the marlin being hoisted as he answers. "Used a naked horse-ballyhoo rig at first. Can't trust 'em, a bitch getting a solid hook setup. Kept losing fish all morning. Switched over to a braided polyethylene ballyhoo lead with a J-hook lure and no skirt attached. Nailed her."

"That polyethylene lead is stronger than steel. No wonder you campaigned in such a whopper."

"I'm not out there fun-fishing to catch and release, like you timid old-timers and castrated ecology boys."

The chained marlin reaches the top of the scale. A white arrow spins in a circle around painted numbers and stops on the weight of the marlin. The fishermen all exhale in surprise. Big moans with disappointment.

The craggy old fisherman turns to Big. "Missed the record by only twelve pounds. Rare to catch 'em that big here—they've been fished out. Offshore of Cuba, yeah, maybe you can still reel in a whopper like this, but not around Key West. You should mount it, display it in the hotel lobby of your new Neptune Bay Resort."

Big stares at the marlin swaying on the pulley chain.

He pulls off his cap and runs his hand over his head, slicking back his dyed blond hair. He claps the cap back on his head. "I only mount record breakers. I'll have her chopped up so nobody else can claim her."

The old fisherman shakes his head in dismay. "Shame to do that. She's a seven-hundred-pound beauty. You should have released her if you weren't going to keep her. That would've been the sporting thing to do."

"Don't talk to me about sport, old man. It's not about sport. It's about winning."

The old fisherman fixes his crinkly gaze on Big. "I been around a long time. I seen things. That fish is bigger than the record breaker Hemingway caught between Key West and Cuba back in the 1930s. Crime to chop her up. Any guy standing here will give you ten grand so's he can trophy-mount her and call her his own."

"I'll chop her up personally. She'll be expensive sushi for the alley cats tonight." Big's broad tanned face breaks into a smile at the old fisherman. "And I don't give a fuck about a fat, bearded dead writer who once caught a big fish in these waters."

Luz makes her way into the Police Chief's crowded office. The Chief, Moxel, and a team of white-suited forensic investigators are huddled intensely over a black micro–digital recorder on the Chief's desk. The

Chief speaks with urgent anticipation. "Just got this—copy of the recording sewn into Hard Puppy's mouth. Could be our big breakthrough."

Luz hunches toward the recorder with the others. The Chief presses the recorder's play button. The recorder's red indicator light flashes. The small speaker crackles with static and the eerie chant of an electronically altered voice.

"Bizango . . . Bizango . . . Bizango
Bizango . . . Bizango . . . Bizango
Bizango . . . Bizango . . . Bizango."

The recorded voice stops. A low-frequency electronic hissing is heard. The recorder's flashing red light dims and goes out. No one around the desk moves; they all barely breathe, waiting for the recorder's dead light to flash back to life.

The Chief slams his fist on the desk, jolting everyone. "That's him, mocking us! Bizango won't communicate anymore!" He turns in frustration on the forensic investigators. "What have you got from Blue Hole?"

One of them shakes his head negatively. "Not even a footprint in the mud was left. Whatever prints had been there were compromised by those damn gators mucking around."

"What about prints on the forest trail? What about prints on the spear shot into the tree? What about prints on Hard Puppy's mutilated head? Must be something?"

"Nothing. It's like he's a ghost, or clever enough to know the tricks to stay invisible. We're still waiting for more results from our lab up in Miami. They're close to getting the true voice-sound identity of whoever is speaking on the recordings."

"The Blue Hole gators? You autopsied them?"

"Killed them and ran tests on everything in their digestive tracts and the feces in their bowels. Everything was what you'd expect."

"Yeah, what?"

"Half-eaten fish, frogs, and human remains. DNA testing shows that the human remains are from one person, Hard Puppy."

The Chief glares at the investigator. "I could've told you that. We don't need DNA mumbo-jumbo to know those gators ate Hard. You guys are way above my pay grade and supposed to be brilliant, but you can't figure out how one guy in a rubber suit is getting away with multiple murders." The Chief fires a commanding look across the desk at Luz. "Don't just stand there staring at me with those big brown eyes. What do you have for me?"

"Well, give me a chance to get it out. I traced all the calls made to Noah's radio show. None turned up anyone who can be considered a suspect. The only two callers I couldn't get a location fix on were Bizango and that Nam vet who keeps talking about Permian extinction. They both were using different public phone booths. I questioned the people at businesses around those booths, but nobody remembers seeing anything unusual. I had Forensics scour the booths for prints. I ran the prints through our database, the FBI's database, even Homeland Security's database. So far, nothing incriminating."

"That Nam vet, he's got me worried. You scare up anything, anything at all?"

"I tried everywhere, even went around to the veterans' bars. Problem is, most guys hanging in those places are so baked on meds they're no longer tightly wrapped. They sent me on wild-goose chases. I never found the radio vet."

"What about Noah? You keeping him pointed in the right direction?"

"He knows what to do. He's throwing out more red meat to provoke Bizango into calling. The moment Bizango calls, we're on him if we get the GPS location of where he's phoning from. Noah knows the stakes."

"When's his next broadcast?"

"About an hour."

"Good. I'll have the SWAT team ready to roll." The Chief looks around at everyone in the crowded room. "I want you all to stay on the razor's edge—stay on that edge until your feet bleed. We're gonna get this guy now."

Truth Dog back on the air. Let me hit you with a pressure drop of info. One-quarter of all mammals and one-third of all amphibians are headed for extinction on this fouled-up planet in ten years. That's a fact. Right here in Florida, we lose thousands of acres a day to development. Half of the Everglades have already been drained and bulldozed, devoured by greed. Check it out. Okay, I see I've got a brave pilgrim calling in. Show me the rage."

"I'm a young mother of three kids; I've got bigger problems than saving mammals and amphibians. I'm terrified about this Bizango character. He's going to be at the Fantasy Parade. I don't care what the cops say about how safe it is to be out, something horrible is going to happen. People I know are scared to death. They're staying home. They aren't going to the Fantasy Parade."

"Not everyone is afraid. The tourist bureau expects eighty thousand thrill-seekers showing up for our annual party. Anything goes at the Fantasy Parade—the shocking, the vulgar, the perverted. If the threat of a category-three hurricane couldn't keep the merrymakers away from the parade some years back, what makes you think they'll be afraid of our own homegrown Jack the Ripper stalking them in the streets? Just gives Fantasy Parade an air of spooky realism."

"You're making me more frightened with talk like that. I'm hanging up."

"Wait! You've got to understand, a guy like Bizango, he has his thoughts banging and boiling in his head. He believes in his righteous crusade. He believes the voices that only he hears come from God's lips to his ears. The problem is, the truly evil ones who walk among us in this world don't show that they are evil—that's why they are so lethal. They hide in the shadows of anonymity, hunker down in the crevices of their cowardice, waiting to strike."

"Now I'm really terrified."

"I'm trying to help you get a philosophical grip on reality. And, uh, one more thing."

"Yes?"

"What are your kids going to dress up as this Halloween?"

"That's the last thing on my mind. I'm not letting them out of the house."

"I've got what they should be."

"What?"

"Skeletons."

"That's not funny! You sicko!"

"Whoops, she's gone. We need a good jolt of gallows humor when there's a killer out there wanting us to jump through our assholes with fear. Hey, pilgrims, you've stopped calling. Maybe nobody is awake. Nobody except Bizango. I know you're out there, Bizango. I challenge you to crawl out from your cowardly crevice. Put your serpent lips to the phone and kiss me with your hate."

At the Atlantic Ocean's edge, Luz sits in her parked Charger in front of the monument marking SOUTH-ERNMOST POINT CONTINENTAL U.S.A. On the ocean's distant horizon, toward Cuba, black clouds obliterate the stars. Jagged bolts of lightning stab down from the clouds; the flashes appear to be a fearsome army of bright giants marching in. Luz looks through the car's windshield at the lightning as she listens to Noah's broadcast.

"I've got a call! Hello, who is this? Answer me! Don't hang up! Why did you hang up? Call me back. I'm waiting. Punch me with your pain."

Luz turns the radio volume up and listens closely as a new call comes in to Noah.

"*Hola,* Truth Dog, brave crusader. This is the Nam vet."

"Welcome back to the show, Permian-theory man. Extinction is your karma. Let's talk about it. It's now or never."

"Do you know how many oil wells are in the Gulf of Mexico?"

"I used to be an environmental attorney fighting to keep corporate-oil bloodsuckers from drilling in the Gulf, so I know the answer to that. There are four thousand off-shore oil and gas rigs out there. The disastrous Deepwater Horizon blowout caused millions of gallons of oil to flow into the pristine Gulf. The toxic dispersants used to break up the oil and hide the crime created a hypoxic dead zone in the Gulf bigger than the state of New Jersey, a floating black hole of death where nothing lives, grows, moves, or swims."

"You've got facts."

"Hell yeah, I've got facts. One of our planet's great fisheries is becoming a gigantic dead pond. And people ask why I'm so pissed off!"

"That's right, but I've got even bigger rage! *Homo sapiens* are invasive predators who are goin' to blow sky-high in a second Permian Extinction Event. Won't even be enough time to load your *Noah's Lark* with a few animals. It's the Gulf of Mexico oil drillin' that's goin' to bring it on. The corporations are crackin' open the ocean's floor, tappin' into a mega-vault of methane gas. Those four thousand oil and gas rigs in the Gulf you mentioned are goin' to detonate at the same time, creatin' a force greater than pullin' the trigger on every stockpiled atomic weapon. And you mumble, don't fool with Mother Nature or Mother Nature will fool with you. I'm sayin', man has fucked Nature, so

Nature's goin' to obliterate man. The mother of all explosions is comin'!"

Luz's cell phone beeps loudly in her shirt pocket. She grabs the phone and holds it to her ear.

The Chief's voice shouts over the phone, "You hear what the Nam vet is saying?"

"I'm listening."

"He's our guy."

"That's not the Bizango voice we heard on the recordings. He's a different guy."

"No. It's Bizango. He's trying to head-fake us."

"Quick, give me a GPS if you've got it."

"Just a sec, something's coming in. He's using a landline this time. We're tracking . . . getting a location. Here it comes. . . . One-four-five Hurricane Court."

Luz throws the cell phone down on the car seat, jams her foot on the accelerator, and roars the Charger away from the southernmost continental point. She speeds up Whitehead Street toward the lighthouse towering above the palm trees. She passes the long brick wall in front of the two-story Hemingway House, where tourists are lined up taking photographs. She wheels the car around a corner and comes to a stop in Hurricane Court with its circle of ramshackle houses. She jumps from her car and looks around. No other police are there. She sees across a dead lawn a shabby house with windows blacked out by inside blinds. The number on the house's paint-peeling front door is 145.

A police car pulls up to a stop, and Moxel gets out. "Hold up a minute, Luz." He nods toward the house with the blacked-out windows. "That guy in there is a psycho killer. The SWAT team is on their way. Let's wait."

"I'm not waiting." Luz pulls her Glock out of its holster. "Back me up. I'm going in."

"That's crazy. The guy's a Nam vet. He could have the place booby-trapped to explode. He was trained to do that shit."

Luz ignores Moxel and runs across the dead lawn to the front door. She grabs the door handle; it is locked. She stands back, gripping her pistol tightly in both hands. She kicks the door, banging it open. She bursts inside a living room darkened by closed blinds covering the windows. She whips her pistol around in every direction, her head snapping from side to side, ready for someone to jump up from behind the shadows of cluttered furniture. She steps cautiously across the room toward a splinter of light creeping along the bottom of a closed door. She stops at the door and listens for sounds on the other side. She hears nothing. She places her hand on the handle and twists it quietly to an open position. She throws the door back, and a sudden burst of light from a brightly lit room illuminates her completely.

Facing Luz on the far side of the room is a man in his sixties, his fierce face etched with a spider web of wrinkles, his large wedge-shaped head shaved; a thick gray walrus mustache hangs over his top lip and down the sides of his mouth. He sits at stiff-backed attention in a battered aluminum wheelchair with worn duct tape wrapped tightly on its two arched handles. A coarse green military blanket covers the man from the waist down. On the wall behind hangs a Vietnam-era Missing in Action flag with the silhouette of a soldier's head bent forlornly in front of a prison guard-tower. The flag's logo declares, in blood-red letters, POW-MIA, YOU ARE NOT FORGOTTEN.

The man stares pointedly at Luz as if he has been expecting her. His words rush out. "Welcome to the Casbah!"

"Police! Raise your hands and put them behind your head!"

The man's hands move quickly toward the blanket covering him below the waist.

Luz grips her pistol harder and splays her legs apart into a firing stance. "One more move toward that blanket and I'll blow you to hell. Hands up!"

Moxel bursts in behind Luz, his gun out. He looks at the man in the wheelchair and whoops. "We got Bizango! Keep him covered! I'm cuffing him!" The man's hands move toward the top of the blanket. Moxel shouts at Luz, "There's a gun under the blanket! I can see its bulge! Shoot him if he moves!"

Luz steps closer to the man, her pistol held in firing position at his head.

Moxel grabs the edge of the man's blanket. "I've got your Bizango ass now!" He rips the blanket away from the man's lap and looks down.

Aimed straight at Moxel are two blunt fleshy stumps of the man's legs, amputated above his knees. He throws his head back and laughs. "You thought I was Bizango! Fools! Everyone with a brain and heart is Bizango now, even those of us who can only dream of what he does! Bizango said to boogie till you bounce, bop till you drop. I boogied in Nam. The parachute didn't open fully when I jumped out of a plane and bopped down; I bounced. Lost my legs. And this country doesn't give a shit now. I'm forgotten history, political roadkill. Just like that Vietnam girl runnin' down the road with napalm burnin' her skin off. Just like that pathetic pelican covered in oil from the

Deepwater Horizon blowout, its wings spread out, tryin' to fly. I'll never be airborne again."

Behind Luz, a stomping commotion breaks out. She swings around as a SWAT team storms in from the hallway. The muscular men are protected by heavy body armor; antiballistic helmets are clamped tight over their heads; strapped around their waists are belts of bullets and grenades. Gripped in their gloved hands are submachine guns. They aim at the legless vet in the wheelchair.

The vet raises his arms and flaps them in the air. His mocking voice shouts at the armored men: "I'll never be airborne again! You gonna napalm me too? You gonna drown me in oil? Bring it on! I'm ready to rock and roll! You chickenshit killers! You won't get him, you know! Bizango is too smart for you! You dumb bastards only know *how* to kill. Bizango knows *who* to kill!"

Light shines out in the night from an open-sided canvas party tent set up on the earth-scraped construction site of Neptune Bay Resort. Inside the tent, a band of musicians dressed as bare-chested mermen play a bouncy Caribbean tune. Cocktail waitresses in fishnet mermaid costumes circulate through the well-dressed crowd with trays of tropical cocktails and exotic appetizers. At the center of the crowd, Big Conch holds court. He is outfitted as Neptune, god of the sea, wearing a toga and leather sandals; a gold plastic crown circles the top of his long white wig. He grips in one hand a pitchfork, its handle and three sharp steel prongs painted silver to represent Neptune's trident spear. He pumps the trident in the air. "Silence!" The band of mermen cease their music; the cocktail waitresses stop and balance their service trays on their bare shoulders.

Big steps to a table covered by a cloth canopy. "It's been a vicious four-year fight. I've had countless work stoppages and spent a fortune on attorneys. I was opposed by every environmental group. Today, the government approved Neptune Bay Resort. Free enterprise prevailed!" The crowd hoots their approval. Big puts down his trident and pops a bottle of champagne. He sloshes the bubbly liquid into a plastic silver chalice and raises it high. "Neptune Bay will stand forever as a monument to my dearly departed partners, Dandy Randy and Bill Warren. Damn, I miss those boys; I wish they were here to share this slam-dunk victory." He grabs the edge of the cloth canopy covering the table. "Ladies and gentlemen, I present the most ambitious development ever built in the Florida Keys, a world-class resort that will put thousands to work and fatten our tax rolls with the fruit of hardworking capitalism, the fabulous Neptune Bay!" He whips off the cloth canopy. The crowd applauds at a fiberglass scale-model display of the vast complex. Big raises his silver chalice triumphantly in the air. "Construction of Neptune Bay resumes tomorrow. I will—"

His words are cut off by the roar of a boat engine. Everyone looks out from the open-sided party tent at the concrete pier jutting into the ocean. At the end of the pier is Big's powerboat, with its engine roaring. Big grabs his steel-pronged trident and runs out onto the pier to his boat. No one is in the boat; its two-hundred-horsepower engine idles with a turbo-fueled growl, and exhaust steams from beneath its chrome spoiler back fin. On the boat's sleek hull the name *Big Conch* is spray-painted over by a slashed red **X**.

Big jumps into the boat and turns off the engine. An eerie whistle breaks the sudden silence. Big looks across the water. There is no one in the darkness. Big raises the trident spear gripped in his hand and shakes it angrily. "Whoever you are—I will get you! I will cut off your head and piss down your neck and have you tell me it's raining!"

A massive redbrick fort built during the Civil War dominates the entrance to Key West Harbor on a spit of land hooked out into the Atlantic Ocean. The fort's towering walls are surrounded at their base on three sides by a deep water-filled moat. The fort's one open entrance is guarded by two large iron-barrel cannons. Police cars speed up to the entrance, skidding to a stop. The Chief and his policemen, outfitted in riot gear and bulletproof vests and carrying heavy automatic weapons, jump from the cars and run into the fort. They race to the end of an arched brick corridor where Moxel stands waiting, with his rifle at the ready. The Chief catches his breath, looks behind Moxel at a six-foot hole opened up in a brick wall, and huffs. "So this is it?"

Moxel nods at the hole. "Yeah, the fort's restoration

crew was doing structural work on this old wall when they realized it closed off what once was a doorway. Probably bricked in way back in Abe Lincoln's time. When the crew broke through, they discovered a passageway leading into a hidden room. They found weird stuff and got out fast."

"What kind of weird stuff?"

"Really spooky. Bizango stuff."

"We got an alert that this is Bizango's hideout. Did anybody see him?"

"I was the first one here, immediately sized up the situation, and issued the alert."

"Did you see him? Did you go in?"

"No, I was waiting for backup."

The Chief grips his rifle in one hand and unhooks the long metal flashlight hanging from his belt as he barks orders at the surrounding men. "Guard this entrance. Moxel and I will go in. If we're not out in twenty minutes, two of you follow us—never more than two at a time. I don't want to lose a whole squad to this maniac; he could be hiding anywhere."

The Chief clicks on his flashlight and steps through the brick wall's opening into a passageway barely the width of a man. He shines the flashlight into the darkness, exposing twisting curves ahead. Moxel follows him in. They duck their heads beneath the low arch of the brick ceiling as they squeeze forward. The Chief stops, sweat pours down his face. "Jesus, must be a hundred and ten degrees in here."

Moxel's nostrils twitch as he inhales the stifling air. "Smells like a sewer. Smells like there might be dead Civil War guys rotting in here. Let's turn around."

"We can't turn around. It's too narrow."

"We can walk out backward."

"No. We're going through to the end."

Moxel slaps at his face. "Fucking mosquitoes. I'm being eaten alive. During the Civil War, more soldiers died from mosquito malaria than were shot in battle. I saw that on the History Channel."

"Keep your voice down. Is the safety of your rifle off?"

"Of course."

"You sure your rifle's loaded?"

"Shit, I forgot."

"Goddamn it, man. Load your rifle."

Moxel loads his rifle in the semidarkness, snapping cartridges into the clip. "I'm ready now."

"Good. I hope this passageway doesn't go on too much farther."

Moxel follows close behind the Chief. The passageway becomes narrower and tighter. They squeeze forward, and emerge into a dark room. The Chief shines his flashlight around the room, exposing old wooden crates stacked along one wall. The crates are stamped MUSKET ROUNDS, BLACK POWDER.

The Chief whistles under his breath. "Looks like we're in a Civil War munitions room."

"Shit! This stuff is so old it can blow if we even talk too loud."

"Don't get excited."

The Chief aims his flashlight at a wall. The beam lights up a giant red **X** spray-painted across the wall. Below the red **X**, on the floor, is a Pelletier speargun. Next to the speargun is an open box full of four-foot-long steel spears.

The Chief shines his light onto the adjoining wall.

Stuck to the wall with duct tape are cut-up newspaper headlines in bold black ink:

SOME SHRIMPERS IGNORE LAWS PROTECTING TURTLES
CONDOS SLATED FOR WHITE HERON HABITAT
TRACTOR-TRAILER RIG KILLS THREE KEY DEER ON HIGHWAY
POWERBOAT RUNS OVER 22ND MANATEE THIS YEAR
DOLPHINS DIE IN PESTICIDE-POLLUTED WATERS
CORAL REEF DESTROYED BY CRUISE SHIPS
ALLIGATOR SLAUGHTER DECLARED A DISGRACE
TOXIC WASTE LINKED TO CANCER IN THE FLORIDA KEYS

Moxel turns to leave. "I'm getting out!"

The Chief grabs Moxel's arm. "You aren't going anywhere. This is definitely Bizango's lair."

"He could be in here!"

"He's not here."

"How do you know?"

"If he was, you'd already have one of his steel spears shot through your heart." The Chief shines his flashlight up, exposing a solid brick ceiling. "How the hell does Bizango get in and out of here, if the outside passageway's been bricked up since Civil War times? Got to be another way in." He points the beam across the ceiling, then down along the brick corner to the floor. The beam lights up an open carton of black micro–digital recorders. The Chief takes a step toward the carton. He stops at a sudden loud clacking at his feet. He jumps back.

Moxel aims his rifle at the floor. "What's that?"

The Chief shines down his flashlight. The slick green mildewed floor around him is alive with clawing orange crabs. The crabs scuttle toward a wide hole in the floor.

The hole is filled with brackish water. The crabs splash into the water and disappear down the hole.

The Chief steps carefully to the hole. He bends over and directs the flashlight into the hole's murky water. He holds the beam on the water. "Damn, now I get it. This hole was originally built as an escape hatch in case the fort was under siege. The hole is on the exact same water level as the moat outside surrounding the fort. That's why the water from outside doesn't flood into this room. Civil War soldiers could secretly escape this room by jumping into this hole and swimming through an underwater tunnel up into the moat. Bizango figured that out and he did the reverse."

"I don't get it."

"Bizango's been swimming under the moat and popping up through this hole to hide. That's why we couldn't find him all this time."

"Let's get the hell out of here."

"I want you to stay in this room. Bizango might pop up from this hole at any moment."

"Chief, I can't stay here. Tonight's the Fantasy Parade. Bizango will be prowling for his next victim. I'm the one who's come closest to capturing him. I should be out there on the streets, hunting him."

The Chief shines his flashlight into Moxel's face. "Stay put and don't leave this room. That's an order."

Moxel's face twists angrily. "Okay, but you're wrong. I'm the guy to bring Bizango down."

The Chief takes out his cell phone and punches in a number. "Damn, it's dead. No reception—brick walls are too thick. I can't get ahold of Luz." He moves to the passageway opening and punches in the number again.

"Line's still dead. She's up in Key Largo at her daughter's soccer game. I need to get her down here."

Moxel snorts. "Fucking soccer moms. They're at a game when there's a killer on the loose. That's why women shouldn't be cops."

The Chief swings his flashlight around to the back wall and shines it on the spray-painted red **X**. "You're wrong about Luz. Sometimes the only way to counter a man's killer instinct is to use a woman's intuition. I've got a feeling Luz is the one who is going to bring Bizango down."

The Key Largo High School soccer field is a sun-parched grassy rectangle lined by wooden bleachers that are filled with parents and supporters watching teenaged girls in shorts and jerseys battle out the final minutes of a hard-fought game. The sweating girls charge a white ball in a rush of running legs and pumping muscular thighs. A scoreboard on the side of the field reads LARGO GATORS 2, KEY WEST CONCHS 1.

In the bleachers, Luz and Joan jump to their feet, yelling encouragement to Carmen as she runs in the middle of the action on the field. The ball bounces off the leg of a Largo player and goes out of bounds. Carmen races to the sideline and takes the ball from the referee for a throw-in. Both teams scatter back into their positions, hands on their hips, breathing hard as they focus on Carmen, waiting. Carmen holds the ball above her head, her feet planted firmly on the ground. She searches the field for an open teammate. She hurls the ball toward the Largo goalpost, and the action explodes into another blur of running girls.

Joan holds Luz's hand and squeezes it. "I'd give anything if Nina could have seen this championship. She was Carmen's biggest fan."

Luz squeezes Joan's hand back. The cell phone in her guayabera-shirt pocket rings. Luz doesn't hear the ringing above the yelling around her; she strains to figure out what is going on at the far end of the field, where the ball sails through the air above the players. She sees Carmen and another girl leap high, their long hair flying, their bodies lunging toward the ball. Carmen whacks the spinning ball with her forehead, slamming it toward the goal net. The other girl in the air smashes hard into Carmen. Carmen falls, her head hitting the hard ground, knocking her out. The action on the field stops. Carmen lies motionless.

Luz jumps down from the bleachers and runs across the field, with Joan close behind. Luz shoves through the players packed around Carmen; she kneels at Carmen's side and holds her by the shoulders. "Can you hear me?" Carmen's eyes don't open. Luz shouts, "Can you hear me?" Carmen's eyes slowly open; she moans and tries to get up. Luz pushes Carmen's shoulders back down. "Don't move! Watch my finger with your eyes!" Luz holds a finger in front of Carmen's eyes and moves it slowly. Carmen's dazed eyes follow Luz's finger from left to right. "Good. Now count for me backward from five."

Carmen keeps her eyes on Luz as she counts. "Five, four, three, two, one . . . I love you, Mom."

Luz breathes heavily with relief. She kisses Carmen's

cheek and pulls her to her feet. The cell phone in Luz's shirt pocket rings, but she ignores it.

Joan pulls the ringing phone from Luz's pocket and answers. "This is Joan. Luz can't talk. Yes, go ahead, I'm listening. Okay, but it will take her two hours to get there from here."

Joan clicks the phone off and looks at Luz. "That was the Chief. They found Bizango's hideout. Chief said you've got a siren and red lights on your rocket Charger, use them and get your ass to Key West."

Thousands of people wearing wildly imaginative and bizarre costumes are packed along the sidewalks lining both sides of mile-long Duval Street. The excited spectators cheer as the enormous decorated floats of the Fantasy Parade motor past. The floats resemble everything from a jet airplane crashed into a mountaintop, to pirate ships with sails billowing from towering masts, to the marble façade of the White House, to spooky haunted houses. From each passing float, costumed men and women fling strings of colored beads and candy to the playful crowd below. Between the floats march high-school bands, Jamaican tin-drum bands, Dixieland bands, bluegrass bands, and heavy-metal bands blasting an ear-splitting blare.

Through the raucous sidewalk crowd, a man wearing a presidential-looking dark suit and a rubber John F. Kennedy mask obscuring his face makes his way. A Franken-stein monster with iron bolts protruding from his neck lurches by the masked man. The monster is followed by a roller-skating seventy-year-old woman high on ecstasy, her wrinkled body totally nude except for a Red Riding Hood cape.

The Kennedy figure looks up to a clattering sound in the sky and sees a police helicopter overhead. The copter skims above the rooftops of buildings lining the parade route. On the rooftops, police riflemen view the crowd through high-powered scopes.

The masked man is banged into by a broad-shouldered drag queen wearing a red-white-and-blue Wonder Woman costume and a rhinestone tiara. Wonder Woman bats long false eyelashes at the man. "Well, if it isn't John Frigging Kennedy, my hero. Don't ask me what I can do for my country. Ask me what I can do for you! It's Hell-o-Weenie. Treat or be tricked." Wonder Woman slams a can of beer into the masked man's chest.

The man pushes the can away and walks on, his atten-tion caught by black-and-white flashes in the middle of the street. He turns quickly to spot twenty men in full-bodied rubber skeleton suits, their faces hidden behind skull masks with knobby eye sockets; they all look like Bizango. The skeletons wear shiny black top hats and tap-dance behind a brass band of bloody-faced staggering zombies. The skeletons stop and toss their hats high in the air. They twirl around on white canes, blowing shrill whistles clenched between their teeth. The skeletons catch the spinning hats as they fall back down, to cheers from the crowd.

The masked man closely follows the tap-dancing skeletons until his way is blocked by punk rockers surrounding Scarlett O'Hara. Scarlett is resplendent in her Civil War–era satin ball gown, flowing black wig, and sequined silver mask. The gang of spike-haired punks are tricked out in black leather pants and steel-point black boots. The punks' faces are tattooed over by ghoulish inked images. The punks shout rude, lusty comments about Scarlett's creamy swelled cleavage, pushed up from the tight top of her ball gown.

The masked man shoves through the punks to get to Scarlett. He leans his rubber face close to her. "Excuse me, Miss Scarlett, you in trouble? Need some help?"

The punks press in belligerently around the man. One punk spits his screaming words onto the man's Kennedy face mask. "Fuck off, dead president!"

The masked man pushes aside the front of his suit coat, exposing the handle of a pistol tucked behind his pants belt.

The punk shouts at his mates, "Motherfucker president is packing! Motherfucker president assassin!" The punks run off.

Scarlett flutters a purple fan before her face as she eyes the man from behind her silver mask. "Mr. President, there's something familiar about you. Do we know each other?"

"Maybe we do. Your voice sounds exactly like my wife's." The man grabs the bottom of his rubber mask and pulls it off.

Scarlett sees the exposed face of Noah. She coos sarcastically, "Don't you mean, my voice sounds exactly like your ex-wife's, not your wife's?" She pulls up her sequined face mask and takes it off. It is Zoe.

Behind Zoe, in the street, a huge float depicts a palm-tree-studded island encircled by aqua-blue ocean waves. A painted wooden sign is arched over the island spelling out NEPTUNE BAY RESORT. Commanding the island's center is Big Conch, costumed in his King Neptune toga, his long white wig circled by a plastic gold crown, and gripping his silver-painted pitchfork trident. He is surrounded by big-breasted mermaids in skimpy bikinis. The mermaids toss brightly wrapped candy to the leering crowd. Big vigorously pumps the silver trident above his head. He gazes down and sees Zoe in her Scarlett ball gown next to Noah holding his Kennedy mask. Big grabs the crotch of his short toga and thrusts his hips forward. He points the trident's sharp steel prongs at Zoe. "Hey, Scarlett, why you with a president when you can be with Neptune? I'm king of the sea!"

Big's mermaids laugh and throw handfuls of candies through the air to Zoe. The candy rains down as a black-and-white-rubber-encased skeleton appears next to Zoe. The skeleton dashes past her. It climbs up the blue-painted plywood waves of the island float and pushes the mermaids aside. It leaps toward Big and rips the trident away from him. It turns to the crowd, the steel-pronged trident held high in its hand. People erupt in panic. "It's him! Run! The killer! Bizango!"

Big yanks the trident from Bizango and slams its wood handle against the skeleton's skull with a loud crack. Bizango reels backward. Big swings the base of the trident's steel prongs into Bizango's face, knocking the skeleton to the floor. Big aims the prongs at Bizango and thrusts forward. Bizango rolls; the prongs scrape the rubber skeleton suit, drawing a leak of blood. Bizango springs up. Big points the trident and lunges forward. Bizango spins aside; the sharp prongs whiz past. Bizango grabs the handle and wrenches the trident away from Big. Big dives toward Bizango. Bizango swings the trident around and drives its sharp prongs into Big's chest; blood spurts from around the embedded prongs. Bizango yanks the trident back, pulling the prongs from Big's chest. Big's breath explodes in a gasping blast of shock as he falls dead at Bizango's feet.

Bizango raises the bloody trident and hurls it through the air at the wooden sign arched over the float. The steel prongs pierce the sign's painted words, NEPTUNE BAY RESORT.

On the street, Noah runs alongside the still-rolling float. He tries to keep his footing in the terrified crowd. He pulls out the pistol tucked beneath his pants belt. He aims the pistol up at Bizango. "Stop! I know who you are!"

Bizango's rubber skull face mask swerves around. The mask's deep black eye sockets stare down at Noah with the aimed pistol.

Noah shouts above the screaming crowd at Bizango, "Don't make me shoot you!"

Bizango's skull eyes turn away from Noah. The skeleton leaps off the float, lands on the street, and races away into the panicked crowd.

Noah runs after Bizango as a police helicopter swoops in from overhead. From the copter's open door, police riflemen aim down into the chaos. The copter's searchlight beam flashes on a fleeing Bizango. The riflemen cannot fire without hitting others in the crowd. The searchlight keeps Bizango in sight. Bizango breaks off down a side street, with Noah close behind. In front of Bizango, a police car speeds up and brakes to a skidding sideways stop, blocking the street. The car's doors swing open; the Chief and his sharpshooters jump out.

Bizango stops in the middle of the street, trapped between the shooters and Noah. In a black-and-white blur, the skeleton races to a building with a sign above its entrance, KEY WEST AQUARIUM. The building's glass entrance door is shut with a padlocked iron chain. Bizango violently yanks the chain, trying to break the lock. The shooters from behind open fire. Bullets zing around Bizango. The entrance door shatters open in a hail of glass shards. Bizango runs through the blasted open doorway into the aquarium.

Darkness inside the aquarium is illuminated by blue neon light exposing fish exhibition tanks. Behind the thick glass walls moves the fin-flick and gill-sucking glide of obscure sea creatures. The tanks hiss with circulating water. The Chief and his shooters spread out and move between the tanks. The Chief's attention is caught by a sudden black-and-white flash reflected on the glass of a tank. The flash disappears. The Chief looks quickly around. He sees another black-and-white flash. He raises his gun to fire, then pulls his finger quickly away from the trigger. The black-and-white flash is a large zebra fish, swimming straight at him from the opposite side of a tank's glass wall. The zebra fish knocks against the glass barrier with a thud, then glides off.

A shooter shouts out in the darkness, "There he is!"

The back emergency door of the aquarium swings open, setting off a ringing alarm. Framed in the doorway by outside light is the skeleton figure of Bizango.

The shooters fire; bullets zing through the air, smashing into the tanks, shattering glass, releasing a cascading avalanche of water and sea creatures.

The Chief runs as he yells above the alarm at the shooters, "Go after him!"

The Chief and the shooters race toward the open exit door. They slip on the wet floor, falling onto broken glass and sliding among floundering sea creatures. The Chief skids across the floor past a loose octopus flailing its tentacles, then bumps to a stop against a twisting leopard shark. He pushes away from the shark, yanks out his cell phone, punches in a number, and shouts, "Moxel! You read me?"

Moxel's voice crackles back over the phone: "Chief! I can barely hear you! I'm in the fort hideout!"

"Bizango is headed there! He still thinks it's safe! Get ready! Alert all riflemen! Shoot to kill!"

At the top of the soaring white column of the Key West Lighthouse, Noah stands on the outside circular iron catwalk. Above his head, the shining glass beacon revolves in the night. He gazes across the lights and shadows of the town. In the distance, police helicopters fly over the maze of streets, searching for Bizango.

Echoing up from the interior staircase behind Noah is the sound of approaching footsteps climbing to the top of the lighthouse. He turns to the open doorway leading from inside onto the catwalk. He pulls out the Luger tucked behind his belt. The black-and-white skeleton of Bizango appears in the doorway. Noah raises his pistol. "It's over."

Bizango's skull head swivels slowly; the impenetrable black sockets of the eyes fix on Noah. The rubber mouth and nose openings of the face mask pulsate with heavy breathing. Noah steps closer with the aimed pistol. "You can't kill every wrongdoer. Even a hurricane can't blow away all of man's evils. This is the end." Bizango's chest heaves. Noah reaches out in a swift movement and grips the bottom of the mask. Bizango's hand whips up, and skeletal fingers grab Noah's wrist in a powerful grip. Noah holds tight to the mask. "Even a hurricane can't blow away all of—"

Noah's words are cut by the clatter from a helicopter swooping down over the lighthouse. The copter's side door slides open. A sharpshooter leans out from the doorway with a scope-mounted rifle and pulls the trigger. Bizango slams Noah down onto the catwalk as the bullet blasts out a cement chunk of the wall where Noah was standing. Another bullet whams into Bizango. The skeleton raises clenched fists above its skull head in defiant rage at the copter; rifle fire zings; blood gushes from bullet holes ripping into Bizango's rubber suit. Bizango collapses against the catwalk's iron railing, struggling to hang on.

Noah, facedown on the catwalk floor, reaches out and grabs Bizango's skeleton ankle. He pulls back hard on the ankle, trying to keep Bizango from falling off the lighthouse. The helicopter banks hard and hovers directly in front of Bizango. The copter's blades whip waves of wind against Bizango, who clings to the railing. The crack of five rapid rifle shots from the copter tear into Bizango. Noah feels Bizango's ankle wrench away from his grip. Bizango plunges off the side of the lighthouse. The helicopter shines its searchlight on Noah. He staggers to his feet, grips the catwalk railing, and looks over. Far below is the sprawled black-and-white body of Bizango.

Noah races down the lighthouse staircase and outside. He kneels next to Bizango. The skeleton's rubber suit oozes blood. Noah leans over Bizango's face mask and hears faint breathing. He takes hold of the mask and begins lifting it up.

Behind Noah, a police car skids to a stop. The Chief and the riflemen jump from the car. The Chief yells, "Is he alive or dead?"

Noah swings around furiously. "Stay the hell away!"

The Chief signals his riflemen. "Stand back! Give them room!"

Noah turns back to Bizango and pulls hard at the tight skull mask. The mask peels off the face with a loud sucking sound. The Chief and the riflemen stare in disbelief at unmasked Bizango, stunned at the exposed face of Luz.

Noah bends close to Luz, trying to hear the words she struggles to get out. Her dim eyes stare up at the beam at the top of the lighthouse; her lips barely move. "Look . . . Cuban doves . . . returned . . . not . . . extinct . . . hope."

Noah looks up to the solitary beacon of light high above. "I can see them, Luz. The Cuban doves are flying. Your doves have returned."

The rising sun illuminates Noah's boat, with its radio antenna bolted to the deck, adrift on the ocean. Inside the pilothouse, Noah sits at his console. He swivels in his chair and leans close to the microphone, his words stripped to raw emotion.

"I've had calls all morning about Luz Zamora. Many of you are convinced Luz was a senseless cold-blooded murderer, a coward hiding behind a mask. Others believe she was a brave avenger, proving that it takes a woman to do a man's job. Some think that as Bizango she only murdered corrupt souls, making her a heroic eco-vigilante defending those in nature who cannot defend themselves. We cannot accept what Luz did, killing those who kill the environment, but we can try to understand. The world our children are now born into has thousands of toxic chemicals that did not exist until recently. Unknown poisons invade our air, our water, our homes, our food, our blood. Luz believed that this environment caused her daughter Nina's childhood leukemia, that it caused her father's lung cancer, that it caused her own cancer. Who's to say Luz wasn't right? There are over two hundred different types of cancer. Who's to say that all of us are not dying a slow death from rancid rivers, poisoned oceans, defiled land, polluted air, and perverted food?

"Luz thought of herself as the ultimate judge, Bizango the great corrector. Her Bizango believed that man cannot destroy his environment without consequence, that a price must be paid, that accountability must come home to roost. The philosophers say that no man is an island;

well, Key West is a real island in the current of the Gulf Stream, it is affected by the totality of the biodiversity swirling around it in air and water. Each and every one of us is no different; no matter where we are on this earth, we are all islands affected by civilization's implacable currents of consequence bearing down on us."

Noah stops. He picks up a can of Red Bull from the console and takes a long swig. He leans forward toward the microphone, his voice thickening with conviction.

"Loyal pilgrims, the feds are about to shut down my radio broadcasts, but they aren't shutting me up. Don't despair, I remain your Truth Dog, an old dog with new tricks. I've been reinstated as an attorney; my battles now will be in the halls of justice. I intend to fight on as another kind of corrector—a small one, not a great one. I believe that it will take millions of small correctors to defeat the great injustices surrounding us. I leave you today with words of wisdom from a poet back in the 1960s, when something new and radical swept the land called the Environmental Movement. The Movement's true believers carried the torch forward as today's Green Movement, the New Ecology, or whatever the hell name is slapped on it. The 1960s poet sang his words as if each one was a razor blade cutting his throat with its truth. His was a final cri de coeur, a fierce lament of human frailty. He knew in the end we must lay down the sword after the war is over. I'll play the poet's song. I bid you all farewell until my next and very last broadcast."

Noah pushes a disc into the CD player on the console. From the big battered wood speakers, the song of the poet plays in an undulating rhythm, its words smoldering on the surface.

"This old world
may never change
The way it's been
And all the ways of war
Can't change it
back again

I'm not the one
to tell
this world
How to get along
I only know the peace
will come
When
all hate is gone
I been searchin'
for the dolphins
in the sea.
And sometimes I wonder
Do you ever
think of me"

The words fade away, and Noah switches off the speakers. He pushes his chair back, closes his eyes tight, and sits in silence. The trawler sways gently. He opens his eyes and looks down at Chicken, resting at his feet.

"Come on, lover boy, let's take a breather."

The dog trots after Noah out onto the deck of the boat, into the fresh salty air. Noah blinks in the bright sunlight. There are no white cumulus clouds as big as Spanish galleons sailing through the sky. There are no spread-wing seabirds skimming across the vast ocean's blue surface. All is empty, except for a black dot on the far horizon. The dot grows larger as it gets closer, then comes into focus, revealing itself as a speeding Sea Ray boat.

The boat's twenty-four-foot hull skips over the water. It comes alongside Noah's trawler and pulls up. Zoe stands at the stainless-steel wheel of the helm. She turns off the engine and calls to Noah on his deck:

"There's something stuck in a bottle that belongs to me. Will you help get it out?"

She tosses up an empty corked rum bottle and he catches it. She pulls off her sunglasses; her blue eyes are gazing. "So, pirate, what do you think?"

Noah tips the bottle up to the globe of sun. Inside the glass shines Zoe's gold wedding ring. He uncorks the bottle and taps the ring out into his open palm. He closes the ring in a tight fist and stares at her. "What do I think?"

"Yeah, you're supposed to be a lawyer, a smart guy."

Noah reaches down and pulls Zoe up onto his boat. He holds her tight, his words close.

"I don't think. I know: the pirate has his treasure back."

Is anyone awake? This is Truth Dog speaking to you for the last time from pirate-radio boat *Noah's Lark*. Do you hear me? I'm on the line for you. I'm on the hook. I don't want it to end this way. We can do better.

Call me before it is too late. The whole democracy idea in the beginning was to reinvent, to shed the skin of xenophobia, to climb that noble mountain and plant a flag of infinite possibilities for a new tribe. High hopes are these, my pilgrims, the dreams and schemes of those mad merrymakers, our Founding Fathers. Call Truth Dog. Tell him how lightning strikes you between the eyes and you see the flash of revelation across the ocean. This is your last chance. Rise and shine.

Are

       you

               out

                    there?

A NOTE ON THE TYPE

The text of this book was composed in Melior, a typeface designed by Hermann Zapf and issued in 1952. Born in Nuremberg, Germany, in 1918, Zapf has been a strong influence in printing since 1939. Melior, like Times Roman (another popular twentieth-century typeface), was created specifically for use in newspaper composition. With this functional end in mind, Zapf nonetheless chose to base the proportions of his letterforms on those of the golden section. The result is a typeface of unusual strength and surpassing subtlety.

Typeset by Scribe, Philadelphia, Pennsylvania
Printed and bound by R. R. Donnelley,
Harrisonburg, Virginia
Designed by Iris Weinstein